Oscar Wilde

# Shakespeariana

Oscar Wilde

**Shakespeariana**

ISBN/EAN: 9783337058074

Printed in Europe, USA, Canada, Australia, Japan

Cover: Foto ©Andreas Hilbeck / pixelio.de

More available books at **www.hansebooks.com**

# SHAKESPEARIANA

NO. XVIII. JUNE—1885. VOL. II.

## CONTENTS.



PHILADELPHIA:
LEONARD SCOTT PUBLICATION COMPANY,
1104 WALNUT STREET.

# A PHYSICIAN ON LADIES' DRESS.

Dr. Thomason, in an interesting article on women's dress in the Edinburg *Medical News*, says that nine-tenths of the diseases peculiar to women can be traced directly to the wearing of bustles made of heavy heating materials.

The wearing of bustles is unfortunately a matter of necessity from the peculiar fashion in which at the present time ladies' skirts are made, but it is not necessary that these should be padded with horse hair or cotton, but should be made of open work that without being weighty will hold the dress away from the body, allowing a free circulation of air and thus tending to prevent rather than aid perspiration.

Dr. Thomason says that there need be no trouble in the manufacture of bustles coming up to these requirements as it only needs an adaptation of the woven wire pillow now being used in the hospitals.

These wire pillows are woven by machinery from untempered watch spring wire, and are afterwards tempered, making the most luxurious pillow imaginable for persons who prespire from the use of feather or hair pillows and also for patients with brain fever, typhoid fever, or from epileptic persons who are sometimes smothered by turning over during a spasm and suffocated by laying with their baces buried in a feather pillow.

A woven wire bustle made on the same principle would weigh but two or three ounces, would retain their shape on account of the wonderful degree of tempering which wire made from watch spring steel will take, and would also make an elastic cushion support for the back when sitting.

The eminent doctor also states that there is not enough attention given to the manufacturing of articles designed for the comfort of women :—while inventions to lighten men's labor and tend to the comfort of men are of almost daily occurrence, women are comparatively negected. Clothes wringers and sewing machines the Doctor says are very well as far as they go, but he rather laughs at the idea that women should be satisfied with two improvements for them while men are on the look out for things to lighten them in every department of man's labor. This the Doctor, although wrongly we think, blames women themselves for; he says that his practice, which extends among all ranks of society, for he is connected with more than one charitable organization, enables him to make inquiry among women of all classes, and that he finds the most startling apathy among them all on the subject of improvements in their houses, in fact he comes out flat-footed in saying that women as a class as far as his observation goes, seem to be constitutionally opposed to trying new ideas. There does seem to be no reason why women should not find their washing, ironing, dish-washing, sweeping and other household duties lightened by modern science, and women should certainly eagerly welcome and try everything that comes across their notice that promises them relief from hard work.

# SHAKESPEARE AND STAGE COSTUME.

In many of the somewhat violent attacks which have recently been made on that splendour of mounting which now characterises our Shakespearian revivals in England, it seems to have been tacitly assumed by the critics that Shakespeare himself was more or less indifferent to the costume of his actors, and that, could he see Mr. Irving's production of his *Much Ado about Nothing* or Mr. Wilson Barrett's setting of his *Hamlet*, he would probably say that the play, and the play only, is the thing, and that everything else is leather and prunella. While, as regards any historical accuracy in dress, Lord Lytton, in an article in this Review, has laid it down as a dogma of art that archæology is entirely out of place in any play of Shakespeare's, and that the attempt to introduce it is one of the stupidest pedantries of an age of prigs.

Lord Lytton's position I will examine later on; but, as regards the theory that Shakespeare did not busy himself much about the costume-wardrobe of his theatre, anybody who cares to study Shakespeare's method will see that there is absolutely no dramatist of the French, English or Athenian stage who relies so much for his effects on the dress of his actors as Shakespeare does himself.

Knowing how the public is always fascinated by beauty of costume, he constantly introduces into his plays masques and dances, merely for the sake of the pleasure which they give the eye; and we have still his stage-directions for the three great processions in *Henry the Eighth*, directions which are characterised by the most extraordinary elaborateness of detail down to the collars of S.S. and the pearls in Anne Boleyn's hair. Indeed it would be quite easy for a modern manager to reproduce these pageants absolutely as Shakespeare designed them; and so accurate were they that one of the Court officials of the time, writing an account of the last performance of the play at the Globe Theatre to a friend, actually complains of their realistic character—notably of the production on the stage of the Knights of the Garter in the robes and insignia of the order—as being calculated to bring ridicule on the real ceremonies;[1] much in the same spirit in which the French Government, some time ago, prohibited that

[1] *Reliquiæ Wottonianæ.*

delightful actor, M. Christian, from appearing in uniform, on the plea that it was prejudicial to the glory of the army that a colonel should be caricatured. And elsewhere the gorgeousness of apparel which distinguished the English stage under Shakespeare's influence was attacked by the contemporary critics, not as a rule, however, on the grounds of the democratic tendencies of realism, but usually on those moral grounds which are always the last refuge of people who have no sense of beauty.

The point, however, which I wish to emphasise is, not that Shakespeare appreciated the value of lovely costumes in adding picturesqueness to poetry, but that he saw how important costume is as a means of producing certain dramatic effects. Many of his plays, such as *Measure for Measure*, *Twelfth Night*, the *Two Gentlemen of Verona*, *All's Well that Ends Well*, *Cymbeline*, the *Merchant of Venice*, and others, depend entirely on the character of the various dresses worn by the hero or the heroine; the delightful scene in *Henry the Sixth*, on the modern miracles of healing by faith, loses all its point unless Gloster is in black and scarlet; and the *dénoûment* of the *Merry Wives of Windsor* hinges on the colour of Anne Page's gown. As for the uses Shakespeare makes of disguises the instances are almost numberless. Posthumus hides his passion under a peasant's garb, and Edgar his pride beneath an idiot's rags; Jessica flees from her father's house in a boy's dress, and Julia ties up her yellow hair in fantastic love-knots, and dons hose and doublet; Henry the Eighth woos his lady as a shepherd, and Romeo his as a pilgrim; Prince Hal and Poins appear first as footpads in buckram suits, and then in white aprons and leather jerkins as the waiters in a tavern: and as for Falstaff, does he not come on as a highwayman, as an old woman, as Herne the hunter, and as the clothes going to the laundry?

Nor are the examples of the employment of costume as a means of intensifying dramatic situations less numerous. After the slaughter of Duncan, Macbeth appears in his night-gown as if aroused from sleep; Timon ends in rags the play he had begun in splendour; Richard flatters the London citizens in a suit of mean and shabby armour, and, as soon as he has stepped in blood to the throne, marches through the streets in crown and George and Garter; the climax of the *Tempest* is reached when Prospero, throwing off his enchanter's robe, sends Ariel for his hat and rapier, and shows himself as the great Italian Duke; the very Ghost in *Hamlet* changes his mystical apparel to produce different effects; and as for Juliet, a modern playwright would probably have lain her out in her shroud, and made the scene a scene of horror merely, but Shakespeare arrays her in rich and gorgeous raiment, whose loveliness makes the vault 'a feasting presence full of light,' turns the tomb into a bridal chamber, and gives the cue and motive for Romeo's speech of the triumph of Love over Life, and of Beauty over Death.

Even small details of dress, such as the colour of a major-domo's stockings, the pattern on a wife's handkerchief, the sleeve of a young soldier, and a fashionable woman's bonnets, become in Shakespeare's hands points of actual dramatic importance, and by some of them the action of the play in question is conditioned absolutely. Many other dramatists have availed themselves of costume as a method of expressing directly to the audience the character of a person on his entrance, though hardly so brilliantly as Shakespeare has done in the case of the dandy Parolles, whose dress, by the way, only an archæologist can understand; the fun of a master and servant exchanging coats in presence of the audience, of shipwrecked sailors squabbling over the division of a lot of fine clothes, and of a tinker dressed up like a duke when he is in his cups, may be regarded as part of that great career which costume has always played in comedy from the time of Aristophanes down to Mr. Gilbert: but nobody from the mere details of apparel and adornment has ever drawn such irony of situation, such immediate and tragic effect, such pity and such pathos, as Shakespeare himself has. Armed cap-à-pié, the dead King stalks on the battlements of Elsinore because all is not right with Denmark; Shylock's Jewish gaberdine is part of the stigma under which he writhes; Arthur begging for his life can think of no better plea than the handkerchief he had given Hubert—

Have you the heart? when your head did but ache,
I knit my handkercher about your brows,
(The best I had, a princess wrought it me)
And I did never ask it you again.

And Orlando's blood-stained napkin strikes the first sombre note in that exquisite woodland idyll, and shows us the depth of feeling that underlies Rosalind's comedy.

Last night 'twas on my arm; I kissed it;
I hope it be not gone to tell my lord
That I kiss aught but he,

says Imogen, jesting on the loss of the bracelet which was already on its way to Rome to rob her of her husband's faith; the little Prince passing to the Tower plays with the dagger in his uncle's girdle; Duncan sends a ring to Lady Macbeth the night of his murder, and the ring of Portia turns the tragedy of the merchant into a wife's comedy. The great rebel York dies with a paper crown on his head; Hamlet's black suit is a kind of colour-motive in the piece, like the mourning of Chimène in the *Cid*; and the climax of Antony's speech is the production of Cæsar's cloak:—

If you have tears, prepare to shed them now
You all do know this mantle: I remember
The first time ever Cæsar put it on.
'Twas on a summer's evening, in his tent,
The day he overcame the Nervii.—

> Look! in this place ran Cassius' dagger through:
> See, what a rent the envious Casca made:
> Through this the well-beloved Brutus stabbed. . . .
> Kind souls, what, weep you when you but behold
> Our Cæsar's vesture wounded?

The flowers which Ophelia carries with her in her madness are as pathetic as the violets that blossom on a grave; the effect of Lear's wandering on the heath is intensified beyond words by his fantastic attire; and when Cloten, stung by the taunt of that simile which his sister draws from her husband's raiment, arrays himself in that husband's very garb to work upon her the deed of shame, we feel that there is nothing in the whole of modern French realism, nothing even in *Thérèse Raquin*, that masterpiece of horror, which for terrible and tragic significance can compare with that strange scene in *Cymbeline*.

In the actual dialogue also some of the most striking passages are those suggested by costume. Rosalind's

> Dost thou think, though I am caparisoned like a man, I have a doublet and hose in my disposition?

Constance's

> Grief fills the place up of my absent child,
> Stuffs out his vacant garments with his form:

and the quick sharp cry of Elizabeth—

> Ah! cut my lace asunder!

are only a few of the many examples one might quote. One of the finest effects I have ever seen on the stage was Salvini, in the last act of *Lear*, tearing the plume from Kent's cap and applying it to Cordelia's lips when he came to the line,

> This feather stirs; she lives!

Mr. Booth, whose Lear has many noble qualities of passion, plucked, I remember, some fur from his archæologically-incorrect ermine for the same business; but Salvini's was the finer effect of the two, as well as the truer. And those who saw Mr. Irving in the last act of *Richard the Third* have not, I am sure, forgotten how much the agony and terror of his dream was intensified, by contrast, through the calm and quiet that preceded it, and the delivery of such lines as

> What, is my beaver easier than it was?
> And all my armour laid into my tent?
> Look that my staves be sound and not too heavy—

lines which had a double meaning for the audience, remembering the last words which Richard's mother called after him as he was marching to Bosworth:

> Therefore take with thee my most grievous curse,
> Which in the day of battle tire thee more
> Than all the complete armour that thou wear'st.

As regards the resources which Shakespeare had at his disposal, it is to be remarked that, while he more than once complains of the smallness of the stage on which he has to produce big historical plays and of the want of scenery which obliges him to cut out many effective open-air incidents, he always writes as a dramatist who had at his disposal a most elaborate theatrical wardrobe, and who could rely on the actors taking pains about their make-up. Even now it is difficult to produce such a play as the *Comedy of Errors*; and to the picturesque accident of Miss Ellen Terry's brother resembling herself we owe the possibility of seeing *Twelfth Night* adequately performed. Indeed, to put any play of Shakespeare's on the stage absolutely as he himself wished it to be done, requires the services of a good property-man, a clever wigmaker, a costumier with a sense of colour and a knowledge of textures, a master of the methods of making up, a fencing-master, a dancing-master, and an artist to personally direct the whole production. For he is most careful to tell us the dress and appearance of each character. 'Racine abhorre la réalité,' says Auguste Vacquerie somewhere; 'il ne daigne pas s'occuper de son costume. Si l'on s'en rapportait aux indications du poète, Agamemnon serait vêtu d'un sceptre et Achille d'un épée.' But with Shakespeare it is very different. He gives us directions about the costumes of Perdita, Florizel, Autolicus, the Witches in *Macbeth* and the Apothecary in *Romeo and Juliet*, several elaborate descriptions of his fat knight, and a detailed account of the extraordinary garb in which Petruchio is to be married. Rosalind, he tells us, is tall, and is to carry a spear and a little axe; Celia is smaller, and is to paint her face brown so as to look sunburnt. The children who play at fairies in Windsor Forest are to be dressed in white and green—a compliment, by the way, to Queen Elizabeth, whose favourite colours they were—and in white, with green garlands and gilded vizors, the angels are to come to Katharine in Kimbolton. Bottom is in homespun, Lysander is distinguished from Oberon by his wearing an Athenian dress, and Launce has holes in his boots. The Duchess of Gloucester stands in a white sheet with her husband in mourning beside her. The motley of the Fool, the scarlet of the Cardinal, and the French lilies broidered on the English coats, are all made occasion for jest or taunt in the dialogue. We know the pattern on the Dauphin's armour and on the Pucelle's sword, the crest on Warwick's helmet and the colour of Bardolph's nose. Portia has golden hair, Phœbe is black-haired, Orlando has chestnut curls, and Sir Andrew Aguecheek's hair hangs like flax on a distaff, and won't curl at all. Some of the characters are stout, some lean, some straight, some hunchback, some fair, some dark, and some are to blacken their faces. Lear has a white beard, Hamlet's father a grizzled one, the Benedict is to shave his in the course of the play. Indeed, on the subject of stage beards Shakespeare is quite elaborate: tells us of the many different colours in use, and gives a hint to actors to always see that their own are properly tied on. There is a dance of reapers in rye-straw hats, and of rustics in hairy coats like satyrs ; a masque of Amazons, a masque of Russians, and a classical masque ; several immortal scenes over a weaver in an ass's head, a riot over the colour of a coat which it takes the Lord Mayor of London to quell, and a scene between an infuriated husband and his wife's milliner about the slashing of a sleeve.

As for the metaphors Shakespeare draws from dress, and the aphorisms he makes on it, his hits at the costume of his age, particularly at the ridiculous size of the ladies' bonnets, and the many descriptions of the *mundus muliebris*, from the song of Autolycus in the *Winter's Tale* down to the account of the Duchess of Milan's gown in *Much Ado About Nothing*, they are far too numerous to quote ; though it may be worth while to remind people that the whole of the Philosophy of Clothes is to be found in Lear's scene with Edgar—a passage which has the advantage of brevity and of style over that prolonged struggle between the Scotch dialect and the German irregular verbs which is such an exciting quality in *Sartor Resartus*. But I think that from what I have already said it is quite clear that Shakespeare was very much interested in costume. I do not mean in that shallow sense by which it has been concluded from his knowledge of deeds and daffodils that he was the Blackstone and Paxton of the Elizabethan age ; but that he saw that costume could be made at once impressive of a certain effect on the audience and expressive of certain types of character, and is one of the essential factors of the means which a realistic dramatist has at his disposal. Indeed to him the deformed figure of Richard was of as much value as Juliet's loveliness ; he sets the serge of the radical beside the silks of the lord, and sees the stage effects to be got from both ; he has as much delight in Caliban as he has in Ariel, in rags as he has in cloth of gold, and recognises the artistic beauty of ugliness.

The difficulty Ducis felt about translating *Othello* in consequence of the importance given to such a vulgar thing as a handkerchief, and his attempt to soften its grossness by making the Moor reiterate, 'Le bandeau ! le bandeau !' may be taken as an example of the difference between *la tragédie philosophique* and the drama of real life ; and the introduction for the first time of the word *mouchoir* at the Théâtre Français was an era in that romantic-realistic movement of which Hugo is the father and M. Zola the *enfant terrible*. Just as the classicism of the earlier part of the century was emphasised by Talma's refusal to play Greek heroes any longer in a powdered periwig—one of the many instances, by the way, of the desire for archæological accuracy in dress which has distinguished the great actors of our age.

In criticising the importance given to money in *La Comédie*

*Humaine*, Théophile Gautier says that Balzac may claim to have invented a new hero in fiction, *le héros métallique*. Of Shakespeare it may be said that he was the first to see the dramatic value of doublets, and that a climax may depend on a crinoline.

The burning of the Globe Theatre—an event, by the way, due to the realism of Shakespeare's stage management—has unfortunately robbed us of many important documents; but in the inventory, still in existence, of the costume wardrobe of a London theatre in Shakespeare's time,[1] there are mentioned particular costumes for cardinals, shepherds, kings, clowns, friars, and fools; green coats for Robin Hood's men, and a green gown for Maid Marian; a white and gold doublet for Henry the Fifth, and a robe for Longshanks; besides surplices, copes, damask gowns, gowns of cloth of gold and of cloth of silver, taffeta gowns, calico gowns, velvet coats, satin coats, frieze coats, jerkins of yellow leather and of black leather, red suits, grey suits, French Pierrot suits, a robe 'for too go invisibell,' which seems inexpensive at 3*l.* 10*s.*, and, I regret to say, four fardingales—all of which show a desire to give every character an appropriate dress. There are also entries of Spanish, Moorish, and Danish costumes, of helmets, lances, painted shields, imperial crowns, and papal tiaras, as well as of costumes for Turkish Janissaries, Roman Senators, and all the gods and goddesses of Olympus, which are evidences of a good deal of archæological research on the part of the manager of the theatre. It is true that there is a mention of a bodice for Eve, but probably the *donnée* of the play was after the Fall.

Indeed any one who cares to examine the age of Shakespeare will see that archæology was one of its special characteristics. After that revival of the classical forms of architecture which was the occasion of the Renaissance, and the printing at Venice and elsewhere of the master-pieces of Greek and Latin literature, had come naturally an interest in the ornamentation and costume of the antique world. Nor was it for the learning that they could acquire, but rather for the loveliness that they might create, that the artists studied these things. The curious objects which were being constantly brought to light by excavations were not left to moulder in a museum, for the contemplation of a callous curator, and the *ennui* of a policeman bored by the absence of crime. They were used as motives for the production of a new art, which was to be not beautiful merely, but also strange.

Infessura tell us that in 1485 some workmen digging on the Appian Way came across an old Roman sarcophagus inscribed with the name 'Julia, daughter of Claudius.' On opening the coffer they found within its marble womb the body of a beautiful girl of about fifteen years of age, preserved by the embalmer's skill from corruption and the decay of time. Her eyes were half open, her hair

[1] Henslowe's *Diary*. Malone.

rippled round her in crisp curling gold, and from her lips and cheek the bloom of maidenhood had not yet departed. Borne back to the Capitol, she became at once the centre of a new cult, and from all parts of the city crowded pilgrims to worship at the strange shrine, till the Pope, fearing lest those who had found the secret of beauty in a Pagan tomb might forget what secrets Judæa's rough and rock-hewn sepulchre contained, conveyed the body away by night, and in secret buried it. Legend though it may be, yet the story is none the less valuable as showing us the attitude of the Renaissance towards the antique world. Archæology to them was not merely a science for the antiquarian; it was a means by which they could touch the dry dust of antiquity into the breath and beauty of life, and fill with the new wine of romanticism forms that else had been old and outworn. From the pulpit of Niccola Pisano down to Mantegna's 'Triumph of Cæsar,' and the service Cellini designed for King Francis, the influence of this spirit can be traced; nor was it confined merely to the immobile arts—the arts of arrested movement—but its influence was to be seen also in the great classical masques which were the constant amusement of the gay Courts of the time, and in the public pomps and processions with which the citizens of big commercial towns greeted the princes that chanced to visit them; pageants, by the way, which were considered so important that large prints were made of them and published—a fact which is a proof of the general interest at the time in matters of the kind.

And this use of archæology in shows, so far from being a bit of priggish pedantry, is in every way legitimate and beautiful. For the stage is not merely the meeting place of all the arts, but is also the return of art to life. Sometimes in an archæological novel the use of strange and obsolete terms seems to hide the realism beneath the learning, and I dare say that many of the readers of *Nôtre-Dame de Paris* have been much puzzled over the meaning of such expressions as *la casaque à mahoitres, les voulgiers, le gallimard taché d'encre, les craaquiniers*, and the like; but with the stage how different it is: the ancient world wakes from its sleep, and history moves as a pageant before our eyes, without obliging us to have recourse to a dictionary or an encyclopædia for the perfection of our enjoyment. Indeed there is not the slightest necessity that the public should know the authorities for the mounting of any piece. From such materials, for instance, as the disk of Theodosius, materials with which the majority of people are probably not very familiar, Mr. Godwin created the marvellous loveliness of the first act of *Claudian*, and showed us the life of Byzantium in the fourth century, not by a dreary lecture and a set of grimy casts, not by a novel which requires a glossary to explain it, but by the visible presentation before us of all the glory of that great town. And while the costumes were true to the smallest points of colour and design, yet the details were not assigned the abnormal importance which they must necessarily be given in a piecemeal lecture, but were subordinated to the rules of lofty composition and the unity of artistic effect. Mr. Symonds, speaking of the great picture of Mantegna's now in Hampton Court, says that the artist has converted an antiquarian motive into a theme for melodies of line. The same can be said with equal justice of Mr. Godwin's scene. Only the foolish called it pedantry, only those who would neither look nor listen spoke of the passion of the play being killed by its paint. It was in reality a scene not merely perfect in its picturesqueness, but absolutely dramatic also, in getting rid of the necessity of tedious descriptions, and in showing us, by the colour and character of Claudian's dress, and the dress of his attendants, the whole nature and life of the man, from what school of philosophy he followed, down to what horses he backed on the turf.

And indeed archæology is only really delightful when transfused into some form of art. I have no desire to underrate the services of laborious sholars, but I think that the use Keats made of Lemprière's Dictionary is of far more value to us than Max Müller's treatment of the same mythology as a disease of language. Better *Endymion* than any theory, however sound, of an epidemic among adjectives! And who does not feel that the chief glory of Piranesi's book on Vases is that it gave Keats the suggestion for his 'Ode on a Grecian Urn'? Art, and art only, can make archæology beautiful; and the theatric art can use it most directly and most vividly, for it can combine in one exquisite presentation absolute reality with the grace and charm of the antique world.

But the sixteenth century was not merely the age of Vitruvius; it was the age of Vecellio also. Every nation seems suddenly to have become interested in the dress of its neighbours. Europe began to investigate its own clothes, and the amount of books published on national costumes is quite extraordinary. At the beginning of the century the *Nuremberg Chronicle*, with its two thousand illustrations, reached its fifth edition, and before the century was over seventeen editions were published of Munster's *Cosmography*. Beside these two books there were also the works of Michael Colyns, of Hans Weigel, of Amman, and of Vecellio himself, all of them well illustrated, some of the drawings in Vecellio being probably from the hand of Titian. Nor was it only from books and treatises that people acquired their knowledge; but the rise of foreign travel, the increased commercial intercourse between countries, and diplomatic missions, gave every nation many opportunities of studying the various forms of contemporary dress. After the departure, for instance, from England of the ambassadors from the Czar, the Sultan, and the Prince of Morocco, Henry the Eighth and his friends gave several masques in the strange attire of their visitors. Later on London saw, perhaps too often, the sombre splendour of the Spanish Court, and to Elizabeth came envoys from all lands, whose dress, Shakespeare tells us, had an important influence on English costume.

And the interest was not confined merely to classical dress, or the dress of foreign nations; there was also a good deal of research, among theatrical people especially, into the ancient costume of England itself: and when Shakespeare, in the prologue to one of his plays, expresses his regret at being unable to produce helmets of the period, he is speaking as an Elizabethan manager and not merely as an Elizabethan poet. At Cambridge, for instance, during his day, a play of *Richard the Third* was performed in which the actors were attired in real dresses of the time, procured from the great collection of historical costumes in the Tower, which was always open to the inspection of managers, and sometimes placed at their disposal. And I cannot help thinking that this performance must have been far more artistic, as regards costume, than Garrick's mounting of Shakespeare's own play on the subject, in which he himself appeared in a nondescript fancy dress, and everybody else in the costume of George the Third, Richmond especially being much admired in the uniform of a young guardsman.

For what is the use to the stage of that archæology which has suddenly become the *bête noire* of the critics, but that it, and it alone, can give us the architecture and apparel suitable to the time in which the action in the play passes? It enables us to see a Greek dressed like a Greek, and an Italian like an Italian; to enjoy the arcades of Venice and the balconies of Verona; and, if the play deals with any of the great eras in our country's history, to contemplate the age in its proper attire, and the king in his habit as he lived. And I wonder, *par parenthèse*, what Lord Lytton would have said some time ago, at the Princess's Theatre, had the curtain risen on his father's Brutus reclining in a Queen Anne chair, attired in a flowing wig and a flowered dressing-gown, a costume which in the last century was considered peculiarly appropriate to an antique Roman! For in those halcyon days of the drama no archæology troubled the stage, or distressed the critics, and our inartistic grandfathers sat peaceably in a stifling atmosphere of anachronisms, and beheld with the calm complacency of the age of prose an Iachimo in powder and patches, a Lear in lace ruffles, and a Lady Macbeth in a large crinoline. I can understand archæology being attacked on the ground of its excessive realism, but to attack it as pedantic seems to be very much beside the mark. However, to attack it for any reason is foolish; one might just as well speak disrespectfully of the equator. For archæology, being a science, is neither good nor bad, but a fact simply. Its value depends entirely on how it is used, and only an artist can use it. We look to the archæologist for the materials, to the artist for the method.

In designing the scenery and costumes for any of Shakespeare's plays, the first thing the artist has to settle is the best date for the drama. This should be determined by the general spirit of the play, more than by any actual historical references which may occur in it. Most *Hamlets* I have seen were placed far too early. *Hamlet* is essentially a scholar of the Revival of Learning; and if the allusion to the recent invasion of England by the Danes puts it back to the ninth century, the use of foils brings it down much later. *Once, however, that the date has been fixed, then the archæologist is to supply us with the facts, which the artist is to convert into effects.*

It has been said that the anachronisms in the plays themselves show us that Shakespeare was indifferent to historical accuracy, and a great deal of capital has been made out of Hector's indiscreet quotation from Aristotle. Upon the other hand, the anachronisms are really few in number, and not very important, and, had Shakespeare's attention been drawn to them by a brother artist, he would probably have corrected them. For, though they can hardly be called blemishes, they are certainly not the great beauties of his work; or at least, if they are, their anachronistic charm cannot be emphasised unless the play is properly mounted according to its proper date. In looking at Shakespeare's plays as a whole, however, what is really remarkable is their extraordinary fidelity as regards his personages and his plots. Many of his *dramatis personæ* are people who had actually existed, and some of them might have been seen in real life by a portion of his audience. Indeed the most violent attack that was made on Shakespeare in his time was for his supposed caricature of Lord Cobham. As for his plots, Shakespeare nearly always draws them either from authentic history, or from the old ballads and traditions which served as history to the Elizabethan public, and which even now no scientific historian would dismiss as absolutely untrue. And not merely did he select fact instead of fancy as the basis of his imaginative work, but he always gives to each play the general character, the social atmosphere in a word, of the age in question. Stupidity he recognises as being one of the permanent characteristics of all civilisations; so he sees no difference between a London mob of his own day and a Roman mob of Pagan days, between a silly watchman in Messina and a silly Justice of the Peace in Windsor. But when he deals with higher characters, with those exceptions of each age which are so fine that they become its types, he gives them absolutely the stamp and seal of their time. Virgilia is one of those Roman wives on whose tomb was written 'Domi mansit, lanam fecit,' as surely as Juliet is the romantic girl of the Renaissance. He is even true to the characteristics of race. Hamlet has all the imagination and irresolution of the Celt, and the Princess Katharine is as entirely French as the heroine of *Divorçons*. Harry the Fifth is a pure Englishman, and Othello a perfect Moor.

Again, when Shakespeare deals with the history of England from the fourteenth to the sixteenth centuries, it is wonderful how careful he is to have his facts perfectly right—indeed he follows Holinshed with curious fidelity. The incessant wars between France and England are described with extraordinary accuracy down to the names of the besieged towns, the ports of landing and embarkation, the sites and dates of the battles, the titles of the commanders on each side, and the lists of the killed and wounded. In the account of the Civil Wars of the Roses we have many elaborate genealogies of the seven sons of Edward the Third; the claims of the rival houses of York and Lancaster to the throne are discussed at length; and as for the English aristocracy, if they will not read Shakespeare as a poet, they should certainly read him as a sort of early Peerage. There is hardly a single title in the Upper House, with the exception of course of the uninteresting titles assumed by the law lords, which does not appear in Shakespeare, along with many details of family history, creditable and otherwise. Indeed if it be really necessary that the School Board children should know all about the Wars of the Roses, they could learn their lessons just as well out of Shakespeare as out of shilling primers, and learn them, I need not say, far more pleasurably. Even in Shakespeare's own day this use of his plays was recognised. 'The historical plays teach history to those who cannot read it in the chronicles,' says Heywood in a tract about the stage, and yet I am sure that sixteenth-century chronicles were much more delightful reading than nineteenth-century primers are.

Of course the æsthetic value of Shakespeare's plays does not, in the slightest degree depend on their facts, but on their truth, and truth is independent of facts always, inventing or selecting them at pleasure. But still Shakespeare's adherence to facts is a most interesting part of his method of work, and shows us his attitude towards the stage, and his relations to realism. Indeed he would have been very much surprised at any one classing his plays with 'fairy tales,' as Lord Lytton does; for one of his aims was to create for England a national historical drama which should deal with incidents with which the public was well acquainted, and with heroes that lived in the memory of a people. Patriotism, I need hardly say, is not a necessary quality of art; but it means, for the artist the substitution of a universal art for an individual feeling, and for the public the presentation of a work of art in a most attractive and popular form. It is worth noticing that Shakespeare's first and last successes were both historical plays.

It may be asked, what has this to do with Shakespeare's attitude towards costume? I answer that a dramatist who laid such stress on historical accuracy of fact would have welcomed historical accuracy of costume as a most important adjunct to his realistic method. And I have no hesitation in saying that he did so. The allusion to helmets of the period in the prologue to *Henry the Fifth* may be considered fanciful, though Shakespeare must have often seen

> The very casque
> That did affright the air at Agincourt,

where it still hangs in the dusky gloom of Westminster Abbey, along with the saddle of that 'imp of fame,' and the dinted shield with its torn blue velvet lining and its tarnished lilies of gold; but the use of military tabards in *Henry the Sixth* is a bit of pure archæology, as they were not worn in the sixteenth century; and the King's own tabard, I may mention, was still suspended over his tomb in St. George's Chapel, Windsor, in Shakespeare's day. For, up to the time of the unfortunate triumph of the Philistines in 1645, the chapels and cathedrals of England were the great national museums of archæology, and in them was kept the armour and attire of the heroes of English history. A good deal of course was preserved in the Tower, and even in Elizabeth's day tourists were brought there to see such curious relics of the past as Charles Brandon's huge lance, which is still, I believe, the admiration of our country visitors; but the cathedrals and churches were, as a rule, selected as the most suitable shrines for the reception of the historic antiquities. Canterbury can still show us the helm of the Black Prince, Westminster the robes of our kings, and in old St. Paul's the very banner that had waved on Bosworth field was hung up by Richmond himself.

In fact, everywhere that Shakespeare turned in London he saw the apparel and appurtenances of past ages, and it is impossible to doubt that he made use of his opportunities. The employment of lance and shield, for instance, in actual warfare, which is so frequent in his plays, is drawn from archæology, and not from the military accoutrements of his day; and his general use of armour in battle was not a characteristic of his age, a time when it was rapidly disappearing before firearms. Again, the crest on Warwick's helmet, of which such a point is made in *Henry the Sixth*, is absolutely correct in a fifteenth-century play when crests were generally worn, but would not have been so in a play of Shakespeare's own time, when feathers and plumes had taken their place—a fashion which, as he tells us in *Henry the Eighth*, was borrowed from France. For the historical plays, then, we may be sure that archæology was employed, and as for the others, I feel certain it was the case also. The appearance of Jupiter thunderbolt in hand on his eagle, of Juno with her peacocks, and of Iris with her many-coloured bow; the Amazon masque and the masque of the Five Worthies, may all be regarded as archæological; and the vision which Posthumus sees in prison of Sicilius Leonatus—'an old man,' 'attired like a warrior, leading an ancient matron'—is clearly so. Of the 'Athenian dress' by which Lysander is distinguished from Oberon I have already spoken; but one of the most marked instances is in the case of the dress of Coriolanus, for which Shakespeare goes directly to Plutarch. That historian, in his Life of the great Roman, tell us of the oak-wreath with which Caius Marcius was crowned, and of the curious kind of dress in which, according to ancient fashion, he had to canvass his electors; and on both of these points he enters into long disquisitions, investigating the origin and meaning of the old customs. Shakespeare, in the spirit of the true artist, accepts the facts of the antiquarian and converts them into dramatic and picturesque effects: indeed the gown of humility, the 'woolvish gown,' as Shakespeare calls it, is the central note of the play. There are other cases I might quote, but this one is quite sufficient for my purpose; and it is evident from it at any rate that, in mounting a play in the accurate costume of the time, according to the best authorities, we are carrying out Shakespeare's own wishes and method.

Even if it were not so, there is no more reason that we should continue any imperfections which may be supposed to have characterised Shakespeare's stage-mounting than that we should have Juliet played by a young man, or give up the advantage of changeable scenery. A great work of dramatic art should not merely be made expressive of modern passion by means of the actor, but should be presented to us in the form most suitable to the modern realistic spirit. Racine produced his Roman plays in Louis-Quatorze dress, on a stage crowded with spectators; but we require different conditions for the enjoyment of his art. Pefect accuracy of detail, for the sake of perfect illusion, is necessary for us. What we have to see is that the details are not allowed to usurp the principal place. They must be subordinate always to the general motive of the play. But subordination in art does not mean the disregard of truth; it means the conversion of fact into effect, and the assigning to each detail its proper relative value.

> Les petits détails d'histoire et de vie domestique (says Hugo) doivent être scrupleusement étudiés et reproduits par le poète, mais uniquement comme des moyens d'accroître la réalité de l'ensemble, et de faire pénétrer jusque dans les coins les plus obscurs de l'œuvre cette vie générale et puissante au milieu de laquelle les personnages sont plus vrais, et les catastrophes, par conséquent, plus poignantes. Tout doit être subordonné á ce but. L'Homme aur le premier plan, le reste au fond.

The passage is interesting as coming from the first great French dramatist who employed archæology on the stage, and whose plays, though absolutely correct in detail, are known to all for their passion, not for their pedantry—for their life, not for their learning. It is true that he has made certain concessions in the case of the employment of curious or strange expressions. Ruy Blas talks of M. de Priego as 'sujet du roi' instead 'noble du roi,' and Angelo Malipieri speaks of 'la croix rouge' instead 'la croix de gueules.' But they are concessions made to the public, or rather to a section of it. 'J'en offre ici toutes mes excuses aux spectateurs intelligents,' he says in a note to one of the plays; 'espérons qu'un jour un seigneur vénitien pourra dire tout bonnement sans péril son blason sur le théâtre. C'est un progrès qui viendra.' And, though the description of the crest is not couched in accurate language, still the crest itself was accurately right. It may, of course, be said that the public do not notice these things; opon the other hand, it should be remembered that Art has no other aim but her own perfection, and proceeds entirely by her own laws, and that the play which Hamlet describes as being caviare to the general is a play he highly praises. Besides, in England at any rate, the public has undergone a transformation; there is far more appreciation of beauty now than there was a few years ago; and though they may not be familiar with the authorities and archæological data for what is shown to them, still they enjoy whatever loveliness they look at. And this is the important thing. Better to take pleasure in a rose than to put its root under a microscope. *Archæological accuracy is merely a condition of fine stage effect; it is not its quality.* And Lord Lytton's proposal that the dresses should simply be beautiful without being accurate is founded on a misapprehension of the nature of costume, and of its value on the stage. This value is twofold, picturesque and dramatic: the former depends on the colour of the dress, the latter on its design and character. But so interwoven are the two that, whenever historical accuracy has been disregarded, and the various dresses in a play taken from different ages, the result has been that the stage has been turned into that chaos of costume, that caricature of the centuries, the Fancy Dress Ball, to the entire ruin of all dramatic and picturesque effect. For the dresses of one age do not artistically harmonise with the dresses of another; and, as far as dramatic value goes, to confuse the costumes is to confuse the play. Costume is a growth, an evolution, and a most important, perhaps the most important, sign of the manners, customs, and mode of life of each century. The Puritan dislike of colour, adornment, and grace in apparel was part of the great revolt of the middle classes against Beauty in the seventeenth century. An historian who disregarded it would give us a most inaccurate picture of the time, and a dramatist who did not avail himself of it would miss a most vital element in producing a realistic effect. The effeminacy of dress that characterised the reign of Richard the Second was a constant theme of contemporary authors. Shakespeare, writing two hundred years after, makes the King's fondness for gay apparel and foreign fashions a point in the play, from John of Gaunt's reproaches down to Richard's own speech in the third act on his deposition from the throne. And that Shakespeare examined Richard's tomb in Westminster Abbey seems to me certain from York's speech:—

> See, see, King Richard doth himself appear,
> As doth the blushing discontented sun

From out the fiery portal of the east,
When he perceives the envious clouds are bent
To dim his glory.

For we can still discern on the King's robe his favorite badge—the sun issuing from a cloud. In fact, in every age the social conditions are so exemplified in costume, that to produce a sixteenth-century play in fourteenth-century attire, or *vice versâ*, would make the performance seem unreal because untrue. And, valuable as beauty of effect on the stage is, the highest beauty is not merely comparable with absolute accuracy of detail, but really dependent on it. To invent an entirely new costume is impossible, and as for combining the dress of different centuries into one, the experiment would be dangerous, and Shakespeare's opinion of the value of such a medley may be gathered from his incessant satire of the Elizabethan dandies for imagining that they were dressed well because they got their doublets in Italy, their hats in Germany, and their hose in France. And it should be noted that the most lovely scenes recently produced on our stage have been those which were distinguished by perfect accuracy, such as Mr. and Mrs. Bancroft's eighteenth-century revivals at the Haymarket, Mr. Irving's superb production of *Much Ado About Nothing*, and Mr. Barrett's *Claudian*. Besides, and perhaps this is the most complete answer to Lord Lytton's theory, it must be remembered that neither in costume nor in dialogue is beauty the dramatist's primary aim at all. The true dramatist aims first at what is characteristic, and no more desires that all his personages should be beautifully attired than he desires that they should all have beautiful natures or speak beautiful English. *The true dramatist, in fact, shows us life under the conditions of art, not art in the form of life.* The Greek dress was the loveliest dress the world has ever seen, and the English dress of the last century one of the most monstrous ; yet the Screen scene from the *School for Scandal* would not be in the slightest degree improved by Lady Teazle being dressed as Chloe, and Joseph Surface as Daphnis, even though Sir Peter's own costume were accurately copied from an Athenian vase of the best period. For, as Polonius says in his excellent lecture on dress, a lecture to which I am glad to have the opportunity of expressing my obligations, one of the first qualities of dress is its expressiveness. And the affected style of dress in the last century was the natural characteristic of a society of affected manners and affected conversation—a characteristic which the realistic dramatist will highly value down to the smallest detail of accuracy, and the materials for which he can only get from archæology.

But it is not enough that a dress should be accurate ; it must be also appropriate to the stature and appearance of the actor, and to his supposed condition, as well as to his necessary action in the play. In the recent production of *As You Like It* at the St. James's Theatre, for instance, the whole point of Orlando's complaint that he is brought up like a peasant, and not like a gentleman, was spoiled by the gorgeousness of his dress, and the splendid apparel worn by the banished Duke and his friends was quite out of place. Mr. Lewis Wingfield's explanation that the sumptuary laws of the period necessitated their doing so, is, I am afraid, hardly sufficient. Outlaws, lurking in a forest and living by the chase, are not very likely to care much about ordinances of dress. They were probably attired like Robin Hood's men, to whom, indeed, they are compared in the course of the play. And that their dress was not that of wealthy noblemen may be seen by Orlando's words when he breaks in upon them. He mistakes them for robbers, and is amazed to find that they answer him in courteous and gentle terms. Lady Archibald Campbell's production of the same play in Coombe Wood was, as regards mounting, far more artistic. At least it seemed so to me. The Duke and his companions were dressed in serge tunics, leathern jerkins, high boots, and gauntlets, and wore bycocket hats and hoods. And, as they were playing in a real forest, they found, I am sure, their dresses extremely convenient. To every character in the play was given a perfectly appropriate attire, and the brown and green of their costumes harmonised exquisitely with the ferns through which they wandered, the trees beneath which they lay, and the lovely English landscape that surrounded the Pastoral Players. The perfect naturalness of the scene was due to the absolute accuracy and appropriateness of everything they wore. Nor could archæology have been put to a severer test, or come out of it more triumphantly. The whole production showed once for all that, unless a dress is archæologically correct, and artistically appropriate, it always looks unreal, unnatural, and theatrical in the sense of artificial.

Nor, again, is it enough that there should be accurate and appropriate costumes of beautiful colours; there must be also beauty of colour on the stage as an *ensemble*, and as long as the background is painted by one artist, and the foreground figures independently designed by another, there is a danger of a want of harmony in the scene as a picture. For each scene the colour-scheme should be settled as absolutely as for the decoration of a room, and the textures which it is proposed to use should be mixed and re-mixed in every possible combination, and what is discordant removed. Then, as regards the particular kinds of colours, the stage is often made too glaring, partly through the excessive use of hot, violent reds, and partly through the costumes looking too new. Shabbiness, which is merely the tendency of the lower orders towards tone, is not without its artistic value, and modern colours are often much improved by being a little faded. Blue also is too frequently used; it is not merely a dangerous colour to wear by gaslight, but it is really difficult in England to get a thoroughly good blue. The fine Chinese blue, which we all so much admire, takes two years to dye, and the English public will not wait so long for a colour. Peacock blue, of course, has been employed on the stage, notably at the Lyceum, with great advantage; but all attempts at a good light blue, or good dark blue, which I have seen have been failures. The value of black is hardly appreciated; it was used effectively by Mr. Irving in *Hamlet* as the central note of a composition, but as a tone-giving neutral its importance is not recognised. And this is curious, considering the general colour of the dress of a century in which, as Baudelaire says, "Nous célébrons tous quelque enterrement." The archæologist of the future will probably point to this age as a time when the beauty of black was understood; but I hardly think that, as regards stage-mounting or house decoration, it really is. Its decorative value is, of course, the same as that of white or gold; it can separate and harmonise colours. In modern plays the black frock coat of the hero becomes important in itself, and should be given a suitable background. But it rarely is. Indeed the only good background for a play in modern dress which I have ever seen was the dark grey and cream-white scene of the first act of the *Princesse Georges* in Mrs. Langtry's production. As a rule, the hero is smothered in *bric-à-brac* and palm-trees, lost in the gilded abyss of Louis-Quatorze furniture, or reduced to a mere midge in the midst of marqueterie; whereas the background should always be kept as a background, and colour subordinated to effect. This, of course, can only be done when there is one single mind directing the whole production. The facts of art are diverse, but the essence of artistic effect is unity. Monarchy, Anarchy, and Republicanism may contend for the government of nations; but a theatre should be under the absolute power of a cultured despot. *There may be division of labour, but there must be no division of mind.* Whoever understands the costume of an age understands of necessity its architecture and its surroundings also, and it is easy to see from the chairs of a century whether it was a century of crinolines or not. In fact, in art there is no specialism, and a really artistic production should bear the impress of one master, and one master only, who not merely should design and arrange everything, but should have complete control over the way in which each dress is to be worn.

Mademoiselle Mars, in the first production of *Hernani*, absolutely refused to call her lover "*Mon Lion!*" unless she was allowed to wear a little fashionable *toque* then much in vogue on the Boulevards; and many young ladies on our own stage insist to the present day on wearing stiff-starched petticoats under Greek dresses, to the entire ruin of all delicacy of line and fold; but these wicked things should not be allowed. And there should be far more dress rehearsals than there are now. Actors such as Mr. Forbes-Robertson, Mr. Conway and others, not to mention older artists can move with ease and elegance in the attire of any century; but there are not a few who seem dreadfully embarrassed about their hands if they have no side pockets, and who always wear their dresses as if they were costumes. Costumes, of course, they are to the designer; but dresses they should be to those who wear them. And it is time that a stop should be put to the idea, very prevalent on the stage, that the Greek and Romans always went about bareheaded in the open air—a mistake the Elizabethan managers did not fall into, for they gave hoods as well as gowns to their Roman senators.

More dress rehearsals would also be of value in explaining to the actors that there is a form of gesture and movement which is not merely appropriate to each style of dress, but really conditioned by it. The extravagant use of the arms in the eighteenth century, for instance, was the necessary result of the large hoop, and the solemn dignity of Burghley owed as much to his ruff as to his reason. Besides until an actor is at home in his dress, he is not at home in his part.

Of the value of beautiful costume in creating an artistic temperament in the audience, and producing that joy in beauty for beauty's sake without which the great masterpieces of art can never be understood, I will not here speak; though it is worth while to notice how Shakespeare appreciated that side of the question in the production of his tragedies, acting them always by artificial light, and in a theatre hung with black; but what I have tried to point out is that archæology is not a pedantic method, but a method of realism, and that costume is a means of displaying character without description, and of producing dramatic situations and dramatic effects. I think it is a pity that so many critics should have set themselves to attack one of the most important movements on the modern stage before that movement has at all reached its proper perfection. That it will do so, however, I feel as certain as that we will require from our dramatic critics in the future higher qualifications than that they can remember Macready or have seen Benjamin Webster: we will require of them, indeed, that they cultivate a sense of beauty. *Pour être plus difficile, la tâche n'en est que plus glorieuse.* And if they will not encourage, at least they must not oppose, a movement which Shakespeare of all dramatists would have most approved; for it has Truth for its aim, and beauty for its result.

OSCAR WILDE.

# SHAKESPEARE AND GEORGE ELIOT.

Shakespeare's plays began a new order and kind of literature. His rank rests not upon his being the child of a drama that came before him, but upon the fact that he is the father of a whole class that have come after him. Nor, indeed, shall we get much light even in this direction so long as we regard Shakespeare chiefly as *dramatist*, the main fact being, as Emerson says, that "he was a full man that liked to talk," that he became dramatist simply because, for the moment, the drama was "ballad, epic, newspaper, caucus, lecture, Punch, and library at the same time," and that to take account of form where such wisdom of life is in question is "like making a question concerning the paper on which a king's message is written."

Looking at Shakespeare, then, from this high point of view, regarding his writings not as *plays*, but as expressions of his mind and art, we find in him this supreme purpose—*to depict life*. Shakespeare enters into the position and feeling of his creations in order that he may portray the motive and life of a soul. The inward, not the outward, life is the theme; character, not events; and the movement and issue depend upon what *that soul* evolves from the conditions in which it is placed. Nothing like this had ever before been essayed; but a motive so noble, joined to so great power in its execution, has been sufficient to give the tone to all imaginative writing since, so that the words here used as descriptive of his work express also the aims of all later fiction, the difference between him and his successors being a difference in power, in method, and, more especially, in *form*, but never a difference in motive. It is not necessary here to dwell upon the various causes that have conspired to bring about a change of form, or to explain why prose fiction in books supplies to the modern mind the same place that the acted drama did to the mind of the sixteenth century. The point is, that here appears the proper material for comparison with Shakespeare, for here is something like him in kind, this is, the modern novel. In its present ideals and in its best representatives the novel not only exists for the same purpose, namely, character-painting, but it sets for itself the same standards:

1. Both alike aim at truth. I need hardly add that I mean not historical truth, but psychological truth; not fact in the incidents, but fidelity to human nature. Both are

> Fictions in form, but in their substance truths—
> Tremendous truths! familiar to the men
> Of long past times, nor obsolete in ours.

By so much as Shakespeare is more unerring in this truthfulness to life in all its essentials and principles, by so much does he transcend all others, so that his creatures seem scarcely less human than God's own.

2. Both alike have a moral purpose. I know that this is often denied of Shakespeare. It is true that he does not reward virtue and punish vice with strict, statute regularity; but when does he ever falter in adherence to the moral laws that govern the universe? It is true that often, as in the play of *Macbeth*, the innocent suffer and the guilty seem to prosper; but is not the retribution that finally overtakes the criminals certain and severe? All imaginative writing that is worth anything has a purpose. Shakespeare is full of a natural morality as implacable as that of life; and here again he shows his superiority; others build their plots upon passing questions of the day, while he builds upon fundamental, human traits that are the same yesterday, to-day, and forever.

The unlikeness, then, between the drama and the novel is one of form and of method demanded by the respective forms—a secondary matter, no doubt, as Emerson says, so long as it is the "wisdom of life" which is in question, but of primary importance from that point of inquiry at which we have now arrived, namely, the different methods of interpretation appropriate to each, the different demands made by each, both upon writer and reader. For the sake of getting at these differences more exactly, let us observe carefully, first the method of the most Shakespearian of Shakespeare's successors (for, at best, their approach to him is only partial), and then the method of Shakespeare himself. Let us compare George Eliot with Shakespeare. Let us take *Romola* and place it by the side of *Macbeth*. Italy in the fifteenth century represents a far milder, safer, more comfortable, but, for the purposes of fiction, far less interesting state of civilization than Scotland in the eleventh century; consequently the tale is far less bloody, eventful, and thrilling than the tragedy. But the underlying theme in both is the same—the ruin of a human soul through crime, pursued, not from an evil nature, but from weakness to resist temptation. This likeness is, for our purpose, all-sufficient.

The time included in the story of *Romola* is six years. In the very first chapter we are introduced to Tito Melema, the character in whom, as in Shakespeare's Macbeth, we are to have a study of conscience. Nothing is lacking of personal description. We are told of the color of his eyes and hair, of the tones of his voice, of the face "as warm and bright as a summer morning," of "the bright smile that was continually lighting up its fine form and color;" we even know in what manner he offers his "dark, but delicate and supple fingers" for a hand-clasp, what clothes he wore, and how even the faded jerkin and hose in which he finds himself shipwrecked in Florence fail to depreciate his manly beauty, but simply give him "the air of a fallen prince." After this we see him daily for some weeks, know just how his days and nights are passed, what impression he makes upon his new friends, hear the barber who shaves him remark, "I shall never look at such an outside as that without taking it as a sign of a lovable nature;" hear the painter, more acute and trained in human physiognomy, wish that he might have his face for a Sinon in the picture of Sinon deceiving old Priam, not because it has a traitorous expression, but because it is one that "would make him the more perfect traitor if he had the heart of one"—because "a perfect traitor should have a face which vice can write no marks on; lips that will lie with a dimpled smile; eyes of such agate-like brightness and depth that no infamy can dull them; cheeks that will rise from a murder and not look haggard." Before long, when circumstances seem to furnish an occasion, and when, apparently, there is no reason for deception, the young man gives the frankest account of his birth and the history of the twenty-three years of his life. He wins his way among scholars by his learning, among inferiors by his goodness of heart, among his equals, men and women, by his graceful accomplishments, tact, and fine manners. We should be stolid indeed if we, too, were not charmed by so brilliant and lovable a being. And yet all the time we are haunted by a faint suspicion of something amiss. It begins at our first interview, when the peddler, finding him asleep in the Florentine street-corner with the handsome ring on his finger, exclaims, "Your tunic and hose match ill with that jewel, young man. Anybody might say the saints had sent *you* a dead body; but if you took the jewels, I hope you buried him—and you can afford a mass or two for him into the bargain." Why should a "painful thrill appear to dart" through the frame of Tito? To be sure, it is gone in an instant, and the usual careless good-humor dictates his smiling answer. Or why should a flush come to his cheek at the barber's allusion to a man's "making a stepping-stone of his father's corpse"? or, at his friend's words in appreciation of the valuable gems saved from shipwreck in the lining of his coat, that these were "worth more than a man's ransom?" But we are not left long in doubt; for soon we see him meeting the "first serious struggle his facile and good-humored nature had known." It came with the sale of the jewels, by which he was master of full five hundred gold florins. He was alone in his room, and stood looking at the money lying on the table, "in that transfixed state which accompanies the concentration of consciousness on some inward image."

"A man's ransom! Who was it that had said that five hundred florins was more than a man's ransom? If now, under this midday sun, on some hot coast far away, a man somewhat stricken in years—a man not without high thoughts, and with the most passionate heart—a man who, long years ago, had rescued a little boy from a life of beggary, filth, and cruel wrong, had reared him tenderly, and been to him as a father—if that man were now under this summer sun toiling as a slave, hewing wood and drawing water, perhaps being smitten and buffeted because he was not deft and active?—if he were saying to himself, 'Tito will find me; he had but to carry our manuscripts and gems to Venice; he will have raised money and will never rest until he finds me out'? If that were certain, could he, Tito, see the price of the gems lying before him and say, 'I will stay at Florence, where I am fanned by soft airs of promised love and prosperity; I will not risk myself for his sake?' * * * * Yes, if I were certain that Baldassarre Calvo was alive and that I could free him, by whatever exertions or perils, I would go now—now I have the money; it was useless to debate the matter before. I would go now * * * * and tell the whole truth." This was his first real colloquy with himself; he had gone on following the impulses of the moment, and one of those impulses had been to conceal half the fact; he had never considered this part of his conduct long enough to face the consciousness of his motives for the concealment. What was the use of telling the whole? It was true, the thought had crossed his mind several times since he had quitted Nauplia that, after all, it was a great relief to be quit of Baldassarre. * * * * * * "Do I not owe something to myself?" said Tito, inwardly, with a slight movement of his shoulders, the first he had made since he turned to look at the florins. "Before I quit everything, and incur again all the risks of which I am even now weary, I must at least have a reasonable hope. Am I to spend my life in a wandering search? *I believe he is dead.* I will place my florins at interest to-morrow."

When, the next morning, Tito put this determination into act he had chosen his color in the game and had given an inevitable bent to his wishes. He had made it impossible that he should not henceforth *desire* it to be true that his father was dead; impossible that he should not be tempted to baseness rather than that the precise facts of his conduct should not remain forever concealed.

Observe how slight was this step on the downward path, and how easy then to be retraced! But observe, also, at what pains is the novelist to leave no chance that we shall fail to note the lesson, at what pains to leave us in no doubt of its significance. She pauses to sum up with this generalization:

Under every guilty secret there is a brood of guilty wishes, whose unwholesome, infecting life is cherished by the darkness. The contaminating effects of deeds often lies less in the commission than in the consequent adjustment of our desires—the enlistment of our self-interest on the side of falsity.

It is needless to follow the succeeding steps of the downfall of our handsome, gifted, well-meaning but pleasure-loving hero; to show how he went on to deny his father and leave him to misery, to deceive an innocent and loving woman by a mock marriage, to betray every trust that was reposed in him. They are all detailed with the same minuteness of analysis; nothing is concealed or left in doubt; the six-years' record fills a volume of five hundred pages.

In *Macbeth*, on the other hand, all the tremendous history is compressed into an hour's reading. Instead of being able to look at the man, his face, figure, dress, accent, manner, we have only his words, and these only at a few momentous epochs, separated sometimes by long intervals of time. All those "reiterated choices of good or evil" which, in the other, we have been able to watch as we went about with him day after day are here seen only as by lightning flashes which illuminate the scene for a moment and are gone again. We know not when the cheek flushed or the frame thrilled with the "first painful suggestion of evil," when the "first serious struggle with himself" came, when the first "brood of guilty wishes" took possession as heralds of later acts. We know nothing of his life in those early years which ever have so large an influence in shaping character, absolutely nothing of his career before the fatal meeting on Forres Heath. All those things which in a novel would have been explained with careful elaboration are left to inference. Hence arise a train of questions. Had Macbeth any thought of murder previous to the interview with the witches? If so, when? Had he had any conversation with his wife about the matter, and was the plan due to Macbeth or Lady Macbeth? Was Macbeth an "ambitious, noble hero, yielding to a deep-laid, hellish temptation"—was he a bloody villain, or was he a mere craven? Had Lady Macbeth fortified herself with stimulants on the night of Duncan's murder, or was she only "made bold" by the knowledge that the grooms' sleep was drugged? Was her fainting real or feigned? her death by suicide or from despair? Did she know of the plans against Banquo, and did she, too, see his ghost at the banquet? Was Banquo an upright, single-minded soul or a fawning hypocrite? Does the play include the seventeen years that history gives to Macbeth's reign, or is the action limited to a few weeks or, at most, months?

Because such questions as these "return to plague the inventor," it is obvious that the drama makes much larger demands upon the reader than the novel, by calling upon him to supply much that is supplied for him in the novel; that it demands from him not only a much closer *attention*, so that no touch or hint or word escape him, not only much more *reflection* in order that he may interpret the significance of these as indications of character, but also another exercise of mind, *imagination*, in order to fill in the gaps and determine the unknown from the known. He must himself construct the physical, mental, and spiritual traits, much as the naturalist must from a dry bone reconstruct the living, moving frame of the animal of which he has had no sight; but with this difference, that while naturalists of equal knowledge will agree in their animal, scarcely any two will agree entirely in their Macbeth or Hamlet or Lear, owing to the variable quality of the imagination which recreates them.

Every play, after due attention and reflection, reveals itself as a skeleton whose substance is known by these signs:

1. The words and acts of each character, always bearing in mind the circumstances and motives which may color and modify his sincerity of speech and action.

2. The light in which each is regarded by others, bearing in mind *their* individual bias as modifiers of their judgments.

3. The author's own view so far as may be gathered from the whole course of the play, just as in real life we judge a man from his general course of action, habit of mind, and modes of expression.

Availing ourselves, then, of such things as these, using them as legitimate materials whereby the imagination may reproduce *Macbeth*, and what do we find? At the very outset, we meet all the people whose fortunes we are to follow; we see them, each occupying his own place and with all the forces of the hour at work, so that, had the play been left as a fragment at the close of the first two acts, and had we been compelled to look at these alone and without any of the light of subsequent events, we should still have had abundant material out of which to construct clearly defined pictures of the leading characters up to that point of time. Indeed, for such a task, I am inclined to think the fragment were better than the whole play; for now we constantly tend to read back into the words of these early scenes the motives and acts of a later time, and in so doing lose sight of what I conceive to be the leading purpose, artistic and moral, of the play—namely, to show the gradual change of character, and by what means.

Suppose, then, we read these first two acts as they were meant to be read, simply in their own light, and how do we feel toward the hero, Macbeth? How does one naturally feel toward a soldier, brave in battle, beloved by his companions-in-arms, admired and honored by his King, tender and thoughtful for his wife, a man of whom we hear no syllable of criticism save that he is "too full of human kindness to catch the nearest (and bloodiest) way"?—and this, by comparison with the rash and fierce passions of the speaker, might not imply any undue mildness. It is when this fine and spirited figure is in the first flush of victory, while the praises of his captain and his general for two successive feats of valor are still ringing in our ears, that we catch our first glimpse of him. It is only a glimpse, but it is a very momentous one, for it includes an interview of a remarkable nature. History is full of instances of warriors and statesmen who, in like circumstances, elated, eager, ambitious, impatient to know the future, have gone to the oracles. But Macbeth had not to wait to inquire of any oracle, for the oracles have sought him out, have even made themselves visible in supernatural shape, have stopped him, whether he will or no, to deliver to him their prophetic greeting. They salute him with a new title, present, and a still higher, the highest in the land, to come. Scarcely have they vanished before their first words are confirmed, and he learns from the King's own messengers that he is already that which but a moment before he had declared, "stood not within the prospect of belief." Is it strange, that anything so singular should have produced a marked mental effect?—that instantly his thought should have leaped to the reflection, "The greatest is behind"? When portions of a vivid dream are remarkably fulfilled, high expectation in regard to the rest is almost sure to follow; how much more, then, the effect of the audible words and visible presence of these mysterious creatures, seen by two persons, and therefore not to be dismissed as fictions of a disordered brain! Banquo is no less moved than Macbeth; he, too, feels,

> 'Tis strange;
> And oftentimes to win us to our harm,
> The instruments of darkness tell us truths,
> Win us with honest trifles, to betray 's
> In deepest consequence.

But Macbeth has a more vivid imagination; with him all things take shape at once; and besides, the promise is to him personally, and not to his posterity. Therefore, while in Banquo the curiosity and astonishment lead only to vague and general reflections on the nature of evil, in Macbeth a host of tumultuous visions crowd and press each other—a throne, a horrid image, a murder, "fantastical," it is true, and he knows them to be so, but yet so clear in his mind that they seem even more real than the actual surroundings. Does he welcome these fancies? Is he blind to their real nature? By no means. He calls them "horrible imaginings," tries to banish them—

> If chance will have me King, why, chance may crown me,
> Without my stir;

would leave all to the future—

> Come what come may,
> Time and the hour runs through the roughest day;

wishes counsel—

> Think upon what hath chanc'd, and at more time,
> The interim having weighed it, let us speak
> Our free hearts each to other. * * *
> Till then, *enough*.

Is this the way of a man loving evil either by nature or by use? Rather, does he not say in every possible form, "Get thee behind me, Satan"? Who of us, seeing the object of our dearest hopes suddenly spread out before us, could do more? Would we not first see only the good to ourselves, and then hasten to consider by what means it could be accomplished? If only by evil means, then indeed comes the test of character. That Macbeth began by resisting temptation is a fact that has been too little noted. In this conflict with himself the victory lay with his better nature; and just in proportion as his imagination was quicker than that of a more prosaic man, so was his temptation greater and his victory more glorious.

But the battle is not to be won so easily. The "supernatural soliciting" has indeed been put to rest for the time, but the ugly thoughts come trooping again at the unwelcome moment when Malcolm, made Prince of Cumberland, becomes another obstacle in his way. Now, indeed, come the "black and deep desires." *Desires* only, no distinct plans as yet, mark that; he is not bad enough for these, he has only "enlisted his self-interest on the side of falsity." And, too, even at this moment, which we recognize as the real birth-date of his guilt, there is still a recoil of his gentler part. He says:

> *let that be,*
> Which the eye fears, when it is done, to see.

When his wife, eager, ready, full of the one thought, pushes aside the husband's loving greeting to urge him to "put the night's great business into her despatch," he makes the simple answer, "We will speak further." Not yet is he ready to enter into her plan, though it demands nothing of him but silence and a serene face. But the wife's instigation has its due effect, and he now yields so far as to count the cost of the act *if* it were done. Setting aside any considerations about a future life, upon which he would take the chances, he sums up present restraints—his relationship to Duncan as kinsman, subject, host; Duncan's own good qualities and the world's consequent verdict; the risk to his present popularity, which he would fain wear a little longer. Not the loftiest moral considerations truly, yet good in their place; not a wholly bad man, certainly, but as certainly not a thoroughly upright one. It is not a high sense of rectitude, but rather a balance of advantages that is in his mind, for he goes on to reflect that against all this he has nothing to offer "but only vaulting ambition." Is it worth the price? "We will proceed no further in this business," he tells his wife at their next interview.

But now he has something much harder to overcome than ambitious longings, morbid visions, or guilty wishes—taunts of fickleness and of cowardice, expostulation, argument, threats; and this, too, from a woman, and a woman whom he loves. More than this, she appeals to his honor as a man. She reminds him that it was himself that did at first "break this enterprise," just when we do not know, but probably in the time long before, when present circumstances seemed so far from being in the "prospect of belief" that no harm was likely to come from even the wildest day-dreams. Yet even this is now turned against him. Would he, then, now go back on what he had once said? Is this the way he keeps his word as a man? One moment more of hesitation—"If we should fail?" The answer,

> We fail!
> But screw your courage to the sticking-place,
> And we'll not fail,

joined to a recital of the plan in all its details, ends the struggle, and, yielding to evil within and evil without, Macbeth declares,

> I am settled, and bend up
> Each corporal agent to this terrible feat.

The deed is done. Macbeth is a murderer. Go again into the

room he will not; look on it again he dare not; is afraid of his own thoughts; shudders to think that not all great Neptune's ocean will wash the blood from his hand; wishes that the knocking might waken his victim. Yet so swiftly does one sin involve another, so surely does never the "assassination trammel up the consequence," that in the very next moment he rushes into another crime as bloody to cover up suspicion of the first. Truly, it is only the first step that costs. In the original plan nothing was contemplated but one murder, accompanied by certain acts designed to avert suspicion; but the moral barriers once thrown down, all hesitation is at an end, all self-questioning is omitted, and hands which have once been steeped in blood do not shrink from plunging a dagger into the sleeping and innocent grooms.

Afterward, with remorseless premeditation, follow the murder of Banquo and the tragedy at Macduff's castle. The Macbeth of this later time is one in whom a continuous course of crime has wrought its full work. All the agitation that filled his mind, all those reflections upon the obligations of kindred, friendship, and humanity, all that horror of the details previous to the murder of Duncan, are absent from his later crimes. The whole aspect and bearing of the man indicate a person long hardened in wickedness.

As a study of conscience, the play ends here. For Macbeth knows no more inward struggles; "direness familiar to his slaughterous thoughts" has deadened him to such subtle tortures; he has "in blood stepp'd in so far" that he is simply hateful to us, and, except for the glorious poetry of his habitual speech, which never fails him, not even during his desperate death at bay, we care little what becomes of him.

Shakespeare was intent simply on showing human life as it is. So was George Eliot. The ways of temptation are always the same ways. It is not in battalions and bearing black banners to proclaim their real nature that ugly suggestions and evil wishes make their approaches, but at ordinary and unexpected moments when, off guard as it were, the man's better nature is surprised and fails to recognize an enemy. If he but so much as listen, the outposts are already gained; a wrong once committed leaves a stain that will not out and furnishes a reason for fresh baseness; a crime which sheds no blood may be more cruel than actual murder. To the Scottish Thane, no less than to his humbler Florentine brother, apply the solemn sayings of the novelist:

> We prepare ourselves for sudden deeds by the reiterated choice of good or evil that gradually determines character.
>
> Our lives make a moral tradition for our individual selves, as the life of mankind at large makes a moral tradition for the race; and to have once acted greatly seems to be a reason why we should always be noble.

Macbeth and Tito are alike because their history is the history of all doers of wickedness. They are, first of all, human—human even when acting under supernatural instigation, human in good, human in ill, human in every incident and relation. To Shakespeare it is due that human life was, for the first time, set in its rightful place as a study of supreme moment. That his followers are to be found rather among novelists than among dramatists, is simply a fact determined by the conditions of the times. If, in the future, they shall speak in still other manner, it will make no difference. They who, like him, though it may be far behind him, have the eye to see, the heart to know, the pen to set forth all the pathos, the pain, the bliss, the glory of *living*, are Shakespeare's true successors and workers in the greatest field of literary art.

QUINCY, ILL. Anna B. McMahan

---

# ANNALS OF THE CAREER OF CHRISTOPHER MARLOWE.

1564, February 26th.—Christopher Marlowe, son of John Marlowe, shoemaker [and clerk of St. Mary's?], was baptized at St. George the Martyr's, Canterbury.

1579.—Easter to Christmas. Marlowe received three quarterly payments of one pound each as exhibitioner at the King's School, Canterbury.

1581, March 17th.—"Marlin" matriculated at Benet (now Corpus Christi) College, Cambridge.

1583.—"Xrof Marlyn" took the degree of A. B.

1587.—"Chr. Marley" took the degree of A. M. and in the same year translated Coluthus' *Rape of Helen* (Coxeter).

1587.—After taking his A. M. degree Marlowe doubtless came to London, and his *Tamburlaine* (in two parts) must have been exhibited in that year by the Admiral's men at the Curtain, as the ballad on *The Atheist's Tragedy** informs us.

1588, March 29th.—Green's *Perimedes* was entered S. R. in the address prefixed to which "that atheist *Tamburlan*" is alluded to.

1588.—*Doctor Faustus* was acted by the Admiral's men. The ballad founded on it was entered S. R. February 28th, 1588–9, and *The Taming of a Shrew*, which contains a line imitated from one in *Faustus*, was in existence before August 23d, 1589, when Greene's *Menaphon*, containing satirical allusions to it, was entered S. R.

1588–89, after December 23d, 1588. Compare "now the Guise is dead" (Prologue); *The Jew of Malta* was performed, but not by the

* There is no ground for Mr. Bullen's statement that this ballad is a forgery.

same company. This play appears in Henslow's list of performances at the Rose, February 26th, 1592 (and thirteen times in all), by L. Strange's players, but the old plays acted by them were obtained from the Queen's company. The plays written by Marlowe for the Admiral's men, *Tamburlaine* and *Faustus*, do not appear in Henslow's list till August–September, 1594, when these men were acting at the Rose and L. Strange's had just left that theatre some eighteen months. This fact that Marlowe had quitted the Admiral's men and joined the Queen's, for which Greene and Peele and Lodge were still writing, is of vital importance for the understanding of the shifty character of Greene's behavior toward Marlowe, yet it has, in common with nearly all similar data, been neglected by Marlowe's biographers. It did not lie on the surface.

1589–90.—Marlowe planned the *Henry VI* series and wrote for the Queen's men a portion of *1, 2 Henry VI* in conjunction with others. The proof of this will be given hereafter. It would involve much repetition of subsequent articles if it were given here. A small portion of *The Troublesome Reign of King John* may also be assigned to him—date 1589.

1589, August 23d.—Greene's *Menaphon* was entered S. R., which contains neither in the story nor in Nash's address any disparaging allusion to Marlowe. The passage usually relied on to the contrary (on "idiot art-masters") palpably alludes to the author of *The Taming of a Shrew* and other writers for Pembroke's company, not to Marlowe.

1590, August 14th.—*Tamburlaine* (both parts) was entered on S. R.

1590.—Marlowe left the Queen's men and joined Pembroke's, for whom he probably wrote *Edward III*. In the first of Greene's *Never too Late*, written before November in that year, we find an allusion to the *Ave Cæsar!* in I, i: "If the cobler" (Marlowe, the shoemaker's son) "have taught thee to say *Ave Cæsar*," etc., says Tully to Roscius, the player. I have searched every play of a date sufficiently early that is accessible to me and found it in no other than this one.

1590–92.—Marlowe wrote *3 Henry VI and Edward II* for Pembroke's men.

1592, September 20th.—Greene's *Groatsworth of Wit*, containing his celebrated address to Marlowe, Peele, and Lodge (not Nash), was entered S. R.

1593, January 30th.—*The Guise, or The Massacre of Paris*, was acted by L. Strange's men at the Rose as a *new* play. Greene's address, meant to deter Marlowe from joining this company, for which Shakespeare was then acting and writing, had evidently no effect on him. Peele, however, did not follow his example.

1593, June 1st.—Christopher Marlowe, slain by Francis Archer, was buried at St. Nicholas Church, Deptford. At the time of Marlowe's death several works of his existed in more or less unfinished condition. It appears from a passage in Chapman's completion of one of them, *Hero and Leander,* Sestiad 3, that the continuation was written in accomplishment of Marlowe's "late desires." He must have expressed these, in this instance, either by word of mouth or, as I think more likely, by some writing of quasi-testamentary nature, which probably expressed his "desires" concerning his other works which appeared posthumously. The known friends of Marlowe at his death were Nash, Chapman, Peele, Lodge, and Shakespeare. Among them the editing and completing of these works would probably be divided. Lodge was abroad, Chapman finished *Hero and Leander,* Nash *Dido* for the Chapel children. Peele, in my opinion, brought out *Titus Andronicus* for Sussex's men January 23d, 1594, and Shakespeare used the inchoate play of *Richard III* as a foundation for his tragedy acted by the Chamberlain's men in the same year. The consideration of the grounds of this opinion will be given when I treat of *Henry VI* after printing the Annals of Greene and Peele. I must ask the reader to suspend his judgment on this and similar opinions of mine until all the evidence is before him. The method of my arrangement is adopted to avoid unnecessary repetition. I need here only point out that the Chamberlain's company, being already in possession of a play on the subject of *Andronicus,* viz.: the *Titus and Vespasian* produced April 11th, 1592, could not accept the extant play, and that the external evidence is decisive against this play being written by Shakespeare; the account of it by Mr. Halliwell-Phillipps in his *Outlines* is not reconcilable with other facts in Shakespeare's career. I may also here once for all say that I wish these articles to be free from personal controversy: the correctness or incorrectness of my results will be abundantly evident from the mutual consistency or inconsistency of the various Annals with each other; yet in the case of Marlowe I must make an exception (I trust the only exception) in consequence of an attack on me made by a recent editor of his plays. Some years ago I suggested tentatively in a half-earnest magazine article that the description of the fall of Troy in *Hamlet* might have been originally written to complete Marlowe's *Dido,* seeing that the corresponding passage in that play was evidently written by Nash. Marlowe's editor adopts without acknowledgment my view of the authorship and describes my suggestion as to the *Hamlet* passage as a "titanic absurdity, gross as a mountain, open, palpable." His own opinion is that the description in *Dido,* written either by Marlowe or, as he thinks, by Nash, was "*burlesqued*" by Shakespeare in *Hamlet.* That is to say that Shakespeare either ridiculed the work of his "dead shepherd" friend, or in the very year after Nash's death, took the earliest opportunity of making laughing-stock on the stage of the work of one who was no longer able to retaliate. I leave the reader to choose which view of *gentle* Shakespeare he prefers.

So few of Marlowe's works were published in his lifetime that I thought it more convenient to put the dates of publication here in tabular form.

| Entries in S. R. | Title. | Editions. |
|---|---|---|
| 1590, August 14th, | 1, 2 *Tamburlaine*, | 1590 (oct. and qto.) 1592, 1597, 1605-6. |
| 1591, — | *Reign of King John*, | 1591, 1611, 1622. |
| 1593, July 6th, | *Edward II*, | 1594, 1598, 1612, 1622 (acted by Queen Anne's men). |
| 1593, September 8th, | *Hero and Leander*, | 1598 (twice), 1600, 1606, 1609, 1629, 1637. |
| 1594, February 6th, | *Lucan, Book I*, | 1600. |
| *1594, March 12th, | *Andronicus*, | 1600, 1611. |
| *1594, May 17th, | *York and Lancaster*, | 1594, 1600, 1619. |
| *1595, — | *Jew of Malta*, | 1633 (acted by Queen Henrietta's company). |
| c. 1595, — | *Richard Duke of York*, | 1595, 1600, 1619. |
| 1595, November 26th, | *Massacre of Paris*, | c. 1695. |
| c. 1597 (Middleburgh), | *Edward III*, | 1596, 1599, 1609, 1617, 1625. |
| 1601, January 1st, | *Elegies from Ovid*, | Various editions, n. d. |
|  | *Doctor Faustus*, | 1604, 1609, 1616, 1620, 1624, 1631, 1663. |

It should be noticed as an important point of evidence touching the authorship of *Henry VI* that the three asterisked plays were printed for T. Millington. The only other play entered for him on S. R. was *Henry V*, and this was immediately transferred to T. Pavier.

*Tamburlaine* was the very first play published that had been performed at a public theatre. For this publication Harvey attempted, after Marlowe's death, to ridicule him in his *Sonnets*. "Weep, Paul's, thy Tamburlaine vouchsafes to die." Paul's Churchyard was then, as Paternoster Row is now, the locality of publishers. Again, he says, "Whose corpse on Paul's, whose mind triumphed o'er Kent;" and again, "Vowed he not to Paul's a second bile?" and finally, he calls Marlowe "the highest mind that ever haunted Paul's or hunted wind." These allusions have not hitherto been noticed, even by Mr. A. H. Bullen, who quotes the sonnets in which they occur. I must not, however, be supposed to underrate this gentleman's labors. We owe much to him for reprinting neglected MSS. and making accessible to students plays hitherto confined to a few libraries. He is worthily following the steps of Professor Arber and Dr. Grosart.

Nevertheless, I can but reprobate such language as the following, applied by Mr. Bullen to a theory held by the scholarly and painstaking Dyce, who stands by the side of Marlowe at the head of all workers in the English early drama, far above all his successors in the same field. "Earless and unabashed must be the critic who would charge Marlowe with any complicity in the authorship of *The Troublesome Reign of King John.*" There are portions near the end of the second part which have as yet a probability of such authorship. I do not, however, now prejudge the question, although I hastily, perhaps, declared my opinion against Marlowe's claim in my edition of the play, couched, I hope, in moderate language.

Of course, in a life on which so much has been written as Marlowe's, much that is new cannot be expected in these Annals. Nevertheless, they bring into strong relief the all-important point of Marlowe's frequent change of theatrical company: Admiral's, 1587–8; Queen's, 1589; Pembroke's, 1590–2; Strange's, 1593. These have been neglected by all his editors and biographers. We shall see their importance hereafter.

F. G. Fleay

LONDON.

---

# A TOPICAL INDEX SHAKESPEARIANÆ:

BEING A LIST OF PRINTED MATTER OTHER THAN LITERARY OR ESTHETIC COMMENTARY OR CRITICISM, RELATING TO WILLIAM SHAKESPEARE, PRINTED IN THE ENGLISH LANGUAGE TO THE YEAR 1885.

COMPILED BY APPLETON MORGAN, A. M.,

AUTHOR OF "THE SHAKESPEAREAN MYTH," "SOME SHAKESPEAREAN COMMENTATORS," ETC.

BACONIAN THEORY—*continued.*

Historic Doubts Respecting Shakespeare, illustrating Infidel Objections Against the Bible. Philadelphia, 1853. 16mo.

Bacon Theory. *The Literary World* (Boston), XIV, 12, 25, 80, 131, 181; XV, 80, 184, 201, 375, 422. Wm. J. Rolfe.

The Shakespearean Myth—William Shakespeare and Circumstantial Evidence. Appleton Morgan. Cincinnati, Clarke & Co., 1881. 12mo.

Bacon's Promus of Formularies and Elegancies. Illustrated and Elucidated by Passages from Shakespeare. Mrs. Henry Pott. London, 1883. 8vo.

Did Francis Bacon Write Shakespeare? 32 Reasons for Believing that He Did. Mrs. Henry Pott. London, Quest & Co., 1884.

The Authorship of Shakespeare, with Appendix of Additional Matters, including a Notice of the Recently Discovered Northumberland MS., with Introduction. 3d edition. Boston, Hurd & Houghton, 1876.

Bacon and Shakespeare. John Laird, Jr. Forfar, Scotland.

BALLADS. (See ARMADA SONGS.)

BAPTISM HOME FAMILY. (See STRATFORD-ON-AVON.)

BAT. (See ANIMALS, FOLK-LORE, SUPERSTITION.)

BEAUMONT AND FLETCHER. (See FLETCHER, JOHN.)

Cursory Notes on Beaumont and Fletcher as Edited by Rev. A. Dyce, and on his New Notes on Shakespeare. John Mitford. London, 1856. 8vo.

BED, SECOND-BEST. (See WILL.)

William Shakespeare and Mr. Francis Bacon's Scrap-Books. Appleton Morgan. *The American* (Chicago) *Monthly*, June, 1884.

BEN JONSON. (See JONSON, BEN.)

BERGOMASK. (See MASQUE.)

BETROTHAL. (See WIFE.)

BETTERTON, THOMAS. (See ACTORS, CONTEMPORARIES, THEATRES.)

Some Famous Hamlets, from Burbage to Fechter. Austin Brereton. London, David Bogue, 1885. 12mo.

Theatrical Portraits; or, The Days of Shakespeare, Betterton, Garrick, and Kemble. Walter Donaldson. London, Varnham & Co., 1870. 8vo.

BIBLE. (See RELIGION.)

BIBLE, KNOWLEDGE AND USE OF. (See RELIGION.)

BIBLIOGRAPHY.

Unquestionably the best bibliography of editions of and works relating to Shakespeare is article "Shakespeare" in Allibone's great *Dictionary of Authors*, published by Lippincott & Co., of Philadelphia, to which work of vast erudition and patience this Index acknowledges its exceeding obligation. (It is inclusive of and a large addition to Lowndes.)

For bibliographies of special subjects, see titles of those subjects.

BILLIARDS.

Some Shakespearean Commentators. Appleton Morgan. Cincinnati, R. Clarke & Co., 1882. 12mo.

Cleopatra's Billiards. A. A. Adee. *Literary World* (Boston), XIV, 131.

BIRDS. (See ANIMALS, FOLK-LORE, SUPERSTITION.)

The Ornithology of Shakespeare Critically Examined, Explained, and Illustratated. James E. Harting. London, Van Voorst, 1871. 8vo.

Folk-Lore of Shakespeare. T. F. Thistleton-Dyer. New York, Harper & Brothers, 1884. 8vo.

Animal Lore of Shakespeare's Time. Including Quadrupeds, Birds,

Reptiles, Fish, and Insects. Emma Phipson. London, Kegan, Paul, Trench & Co., 1883. 12mo.

BIRTHDAY.

The Birthday and Name of Shakespeare. P. Cunningham. *Once a Week* (London), VIII, 460.

On Shakespeare's Traditional Birthday. C. M. Ingleby. *Transactions of the Royal Society of Literature*, vol. X, part iii, N. S. London, 1871. 8vo.

Diary of the Rev. John Ward, Vicar of Stratford-upon-Avon from 1648 to 1679. Ed. Charles Severn. London, 1839. 8vo.

The Shakespearean Myth—William Shakespeare and Circumstantial Evidence. Appleton Morgan. Cincinnati, R. Clarke & Co., 1881. 12mo.

The Argument on the Assumed Birthday of Shakespeare Reduced to Shape. Bolton Corney. London, 1864. 8vo.

BIRTHPLACE. (See STRATFORD-ON-AVON.)

The Hoax of the Birthhouse of Shakespeare. *Bentley's Quarterly Review* (London), XXIII, 279.

Shakespeare's Home, Visited and Described by Washington Irving, F. W. Fairholt, and J. F. Sabin, and the Complete Prose Works of Shakespeare. New York, 1877.

Stratford-on-Avon, From the Earliest Times to the Death of William Shakespeare. Sidney L. Lee. London, Macmillan, 1884. Folio.

Shakespeare: His Birthplace and its Neighborhood. George R. Wise. London, Smith, Elder & Co., 1861.

Shakespeare: His Birthplace, Home, and Grave. John Jephson. London, 1864. 12mo.

Shakespeare's Country. R. G. Kingsley. *The English Illustrated* (London) *Magazine*, March and April, 1885.

BLACKAMOOR.

The Blackamoors in Othello. D. Cook. *Once a Week* (London), XV, 272.

BLACKFRIARS ESTATE.

The Deed of Bargain and Sale of the Blackfriars Estate. Verbatim copy. Appendix to Outline of the Life of Shakespeare. J. O. Halliwell-Phillipps. 4th Ed. London, Longmans, 1884. 8vo.

BLACKFRIARS THEATRE. (See THEATRES.)

Verbatim Copy. Deed of Feoffment from Sir William More of Losely, etc., to James Burbage, 4 February, 1596, Conveying Portion of Premises in Blackfriars afterwards Converted into Blackfriars Theatre. In Outlines of the Life of Shakespeare. J. O. Halliwell-Phillipps. 4th Ed. London, Longmans, 1884. 8vo.

BOOKS. (See LIBRARY.)

Observations on an Autograph of Shakespeare in Florio's Translation of Montaigue, and the Orthography of the Name, in a Letter to J. Gage, Esq. Sir F. Madden. London, 1837. 4to.

BONES, SHAKESPEARE'S. (See EXHUMATION PROJECT.)

BOTANY.

Plant-Lore and Garden Craft of Shakespeare. Ellacombe. London.

Shakespeare on Timber, Trees, Shakespeare's Use of Timber Trade Terms, Shakespeare's Trees, their Legends and Histories. *The Timber Trades' Journal* (London), 1873–1874.

Shakespeare's Garden, or The Plants and Flowers named in his Works Described and Defined. Sidney Beesly. London, 1864. 8vo.

The Flowers of Shakespeare, Fifty Groups. G. Giraud. London, 1845, 1850. 4to.

The Shakespearian Flora. Leo. H. Grindon. Manchester, 1883.

Shakespearian Bouquet. The Flowers and Plants of Shakespeare, with their Scientific Names and Quotations from his Works Wherein Allusion is Made to Them. William Elder. Paisley, W. B. Watson, 1872. 8vo.

Folk-Lore of Shakespeare. T. F. Thistleton-Dyer. New York, Harper & Bros., 1884. 8vo.

BROOCH, SHAKESPEARE'S. (See RELICS.)

BRUNO, GIORDANO. (See GIORDANO BRUNO.)

BURBAGE, JAMES. (See BLACKFRIARS THEATRE.)

BURBAGE, RICHARD. (See ACTORS, THEATRES.)

Some Famous Hamlets from Burbage to Fechter. Austin Brereton. London, David Bogue, 1885. 12mo.

BURIAL. (See EXHUMATION PROJECT.)

BUSINESS RELATIONS. (See ABSTRACTS OF TITLE, DOCUMENTS, STRATFORD-ON-AVON, THEATRES.)

Shakespeare and the Stage. *Victoria* (London), XXXI, 156; *Colburn's New Monthly Magazine* (London), CXXX, 419.

Shakespeare as a Player and Poet. E. P. Evans. *The Lakeside Monthly* (Chicago), II, 73.

Shakespeare as a Theatre Proprietor. H. Wright. *Jewitt's Antiquary* (London), IV, 142.

Outlines of the Life of Shakespeare. J. O. Halliwell-Phillipps. London, Longmans, 1881-1884. 8vo.

The Shakespearean Myth—William Shakespeare and Circumstantial Evidence. Appleton Morgan. Cincinnati, Clarke & Co., 1881. 12mo.

New Particulars Regarding the Works of Shakespeare: in a Letter to the Rev. A. Dyce. J. P. Collier. London, 1836. 8vo.

BUST, THE STRATFORD. (See PORTRAITS.)

Shakespeare's Portraits Phrenologically Considered. E. T. Craig. Edited by J. Parker Norris. Philadelphia, 1875. 8vo.

The Portraits of Shakespeare. J. Parker Norris. Philadelphia, 1885. Robert M. Lindsay. 4to.

# NOTES AND QUERIES.

CONDUCTED BY J. PARKER NORRIS.

[*Correspondents and Contributors in quoting from Shakespeare's plays should cite not only the acts and scenes but also the lines. The numbering of the lines should, in all cases, follow the Globe edition.*]

## "BRAKES OF ICE."*

### I.

Mr. Adee and Dr. Ingleby are very near the window next the morning sun. The line must not suffer emendation or change in the slightest degree. I wonder there has been so much confusion and learned nonsense in regard to it. The difficulty has grown out of a lack of knowledge of ancient terms as applied to the common affairs of men. The word "brakes" is a technical one, being general, while "ice-brakes," or brakes of ice, is more specific.

Among countrymen, farmers, wagoners, and others, in the winter-time, when the hills are glazy with ice and the way steep, they are accustomed to use the ice-brake to retard the load and keep it and the vehicle from overwhelming the horses and driver; they put down the brakes—ice-brakes. It is usually a big, rough chain thrown round the felloes of the wheel near the ground. It is sometimes called a *rough lock*. It is a most efficient restraint and hold-back. How a carriage or wagon would go whizzing down hill but for some such contrivance!

But there are some natures so incapable of being restrained, so slippery in all their ways and doings, that even an "ice-brake" is no impediment; and, what is worse, they are not called upon in courts to answer or by society to make reparation; "they answer none." Others, of different dispositions, are not allowed any exemptions or excuse, even for small faults; they are held to strict accountability.

SILAS H. WRIGHT.

WASHINGTON.

### II.

The able article of Mr. Adee interests but fails to convince those who hold, with Dr. Schmidt (*Shakespeare Lexicon*), that "so much is certain, that the idea hidden in the words '*brakes of ice*' must be antithetical to '*a fault alone*.'" Such views have led the majority of editors to adopt the correction, "*vice*" for "*ice*." Dyce, in note

* See Mr. Adee's paper in SHAKESPEARIANA for March, 1885.—ED. N. & Q.

(37) to *Comedy of Errors*, gives numerous examples where the initial "*V*" has been misprinted.

I would venture to suggest the further correction of *through* for "*from*;" the error may have arisen from confounding the abbreviations *thrō* and *frō*. The passage would then stand:

> Well, heaven forgive him! and forgive us all!
> Some rise by sin, and some by virtue fall;
> Some run *through* brakes of *vice*, and answer none;
> And some condemnèd for a fault alone.

"*Run through brakes of vice*" has the same meaning as (*Two Gentlemen of Verona* V, iv, 112) "*run through all th' sins.*" Brakes has here the sense of *dense growth of shrub or fruit-tree*. So *Paradise Lost* V, 326:

> But I will haste, and from each bow and *brake*,
> Each plant and joucy gourd, will pluck such choice
> To entertain our angel guest, etc.

The use of "*brakes*"=*rank growth* may recall the idea in *Hamlet* III, iv, 150:

> Repent what's past, avoid what is to come,
> And do not spread the comfort on the weeds
> To make them ranker.

*Lucrece*, 603:

> How will thy shame be seeded in thine age,
> When thus thy vices bud before thy spring!

and *Hamlet* I, ii, 135:

> Fie on't! ah fie! 'tis an unweeded garden
> That grows to seed; things rank and gross in nature
> Possess it merely;

and *Othello* I, iii, 322:

> Virtue! a fig! 'tis in ourselves that we are thus or thus. Our bodies are our gardens, to the which our wills are gardeners.

"*Answer none*" is illustrated by *Meas. for Meas.* II, ii, 103:

> And do him right that, *answering* one foul wrong,
> Gives not to act another.

Thus, "*a fault*," in the eyes of Escalus, becomes "*one foul wrong*" in the language of Angelo.

In *Henry VIII*: I, ii, 75:

> 'Tis but the fate of place, and the *rough brake*
> That virtue must go through.

Here "*brake*" is again=dense growth, but it is of thorns and brambles of the outside world, not the rank wildness of an evil nature. Compare (*As You Like It* I, iii, 12)

> Oh! how full of briers is this working-day world,

and (*3 Henry VI*: III, ii, 174)

> And I—like one lost in a *thorny wood*,
> That rents the thorns and is rent with the thorns,
> Seeking a way.

To *pass through brakes* seems to have been a proverbial expression; so Ben Jonson, *Epistle to Master Colby, Underwoods*, xxxii:

> Look on the false and cunning man that loves
> No person, nor is loved. What ways he proves
> To gain upon his belly: and at last
> Crushed in the snaky *brakes that he had past!*

To *pass through* has a totally different sense from "*run*" through.

B. G. KINNEAR.

LONDON.

## III.

Notwithstanding the ingenious and scholarly interpretation maintained by Mr. Adee of the *crux* "brakes of ice," found in *Measure for Measure* II, i, 39, yet there are many readers who cannot altogether agree that his solution of the problem is manifestly right or fully satisfactory. *Ice* has been deemed a misprint, and should probably read *law*. In the Folio of 1623 the word is printed with a capital I; and if in a blurred manuscript the word *law* were written with a capital L, it is altogether a supposable case that a careless compositor may have misread and erred in printing the former word for the latter, as each have the same number of letters and look somewhat alike in chirography. Similar mistakes are not uncommon in typography. The word *brake* technically applies to a horse's bit or snaffle, but here it metaphorically signifies to curb, rein in, check, restrain, restrict. The phrase, "and *answer* none," would evidently mean accountable, amenable, liable—an account to be rendered to law and justice. Compare the poet's application of *answer* and also of *law* and *curb* (brake):

> He will call you to so hot an *answer* for it.

> Their faults are open:
> Arrest them to the *answer* of the *law*.—*Henry V:* II, ii, 142.

> Kings are earth's gods; in vice their *law's* their will.
> —*Pericles* I, i, 103.

Hence we would read:

> Some run from brakes of *law*, and answer none:
> And some condemned for a fault alone;

or, paraphrased—"Some run counter to the restraints or curbs of law and are not held accountable or answerable thereto, while some are condemned and suffer for a trivial fault—a single misdemeanor." The two lines completely harmonize, conform perfectly to the *aside* reflection or comment of Escalus and to the doctrine of the association of ideas connected with the play. If the line, as emended, seems but a sententious and commonplace bit of generalization—a platitude—it must be remembered that it will not be the first time that the poet, as well as other writers, has erred in this respect, and that what may be deemed a truism at the present time was not one in his day, perhaps.

PHILADELPHIA. J. G. HERR.

[In his *Scattered Notes on the Text of Shakespeare*, p. 142, Mr. Herr proposed to read—

Some run from brakes of *grace*, and answer none,

but he is now convinced that *law* is the proper word, and wishes to withdraw his former conjecture.—ED. N. & Q.]

---

## *HAMLET* III, ii, 292.

Ex-Governor Davis, of Minnesota, author of *The Law in Shakespeare*, and a ripe and thoughtful student of the plays, has given me permission to communicate to your pages a reading, which seems to me something more than "conjectural," and against which I cannot conceive of even a "conjectural" objection. Viz. (*Hamlet* III, ii, 292):

After King Claudius has rushed from the play, Hamlet repeats:

For thou dost know, O Damon dear,
This realm dismantled was
Of Jove himself; and now reigns here
A very, very—*pajock!*

and Horatio says, "You might have rhymed." Now, what rhymes with "dismantled was"? Governor Davis says, CLAUDIUS! Hamlet suggested the rhyme, and Horatio was quick to see it. The rhyme, I need not submit, is as good as most, and in speaking could easily be made apparent. It is fully as good as Hamlet's own prior rhyme,

It came to pass
As most like it was,

or his later one,

For if the King like not the comedy,
Why then, belike,—he likes it not, perdy.

Besides, "*Claudius*" is exactly what Hamlet wants his hearers to understand that dismantled Denmark now possesses in the place of "Jove himself." APPLETON MORGAN.

NEW YORK, Nov. 15th, 1884.

## *AS YOU LIKE IT* II, vii, 53.

Referring to Dr. Ingleby's note on a passage in *As You Like It*, in SHAKESPEARIANA for January, 1885, p. 38, it seems to me that Shakespeare wrote:

> He, that a fool doth very wisely hit,
> Doth, very *sensibly* although he smart,
> Seem senseless of the bob, etc.;

*i. e.*, although he smarts very keenly (sensibly) he affects unconsciousness. Or else I would suggest to read as follows:

> Doth, very foolishly although he smart,
> Seem, etc.;

*i. e.*, although he is foolish enough to feel the sarcasm, he is not foolish enough to show his annoyance. H. LITTLEDALE.

BARODA, INDIA, March 8th, 1885.

---

# SHAKESPEARIAN SOCIETIES.

[*The Secretaries of Shakespearian Societies are invited to furnish the minutes of their meetings and whatever is of value and interest in their essays and discussions for publication in this department.*]

CLIFTON SHAKSPERE SOCIETY, BRISTOL, ENGLAND, February 28th, 1885.—Dr. J. N. Langley read "Notes on Some Baconianisms in *The Two Gentlemen of Verona*." Papers on "Proteus" by Miss Emily T. Smith and Miss Florence Herapeth were read. The Society resolved to introduce into their work the plays in *British Dramatists* (edited by John S. Keltie and published by Nimmo) and the Doubtful Plays in the Tauchnitz Series—*Edward III, Thomas Lord Cromwell, Locrine, A Yorkshire Tragedy, The London Prodigal, The Birth of Merlin.*

March 28th, 1885.—The following papers were read: "On the Alleged Allegorical Intention of Oberon's Vision (*A Midsummer Night's Dream* II, i, 148–168)," by Mr. C. H. Herford, M. A., who, accepting the general interpretation of the "fair Vestal" as Queen Elizabeth, considered that the first part refers to the Kenilworth festivities, and that if any specific person is intended by the "Western Flower" the probabilities are enormously in favor of Lady Essex; "A Note on Some Plant Allusions in *A Midsummer Night's Dream*," by Mr. Leo H. Grindon, who looked upon the play as second only to *The Winter's Tale* in the matchless beauty of Shakespeare's references to flowers and trees; commenting upon the "orbs upon the green," he suggested that "green sour ringlets" of *The Tempest*, V, i, 37, was a perpetuated misprint for "greensome ringlets;" "Notes on the Language of *A Midsummer Night's Dream*," by Mrs. C. I. Spencer, and "Puck," by Mr. G. Munro Smith. L. M. GRIFFITHS.

---

NEW SHAKSPERE SOCIETY, LONDON, ENGLAND, March 13th.—Dr. C. K. Watson in the chair. Mr. S. L. Lee read a paper "On an Elizabethan Learned Society." Mr. Lee spoke strongly on the mistaken estimate of the character of the Elizabethan age as being one of tumultuous, ill-directed passion. That there was another side to it was shown by the birth of the old Society of Antiquaries, founded in 1572. Outside the Universities such learned organizations had not hitherto existed in England, though flourishing abroad. The dissolution of the monasteries had caused a complete cessation of historiography; Henry VIII, indeed, sent one man, Leland, to search monasteries and other religious foundations for historical matter. Mr. Lee then described three great antiquaries—Archbishop Parker, William Cecil, and Nicholas Bacon—as three men having a better right to be considered representative men of the age than Greene, Marlowe, etc. The great need of antiquarian study was secular development; it is therefore especially interesting to note the large proportion of laymen in the Society. The list includes every class—nobles, statesmen, and scholars such as Camden and Cotton, together with merchants and small tradesmen like Stowe, the tailor. It was noticeable that English was employed in their disquisitions, not Latin. We find these antiquaries on the best of terms with the ordinary men of letters, as seen in the case of Jonson and Stowe, of the help given by Seldon to Drayton, etc. This may account for the small mention of them in the contemporary drama, as they could hardly be introduced except in a burlesque or travesty of them, which their friendly relations with the stage put out of the question. Mr. Lee then sketched the decline of the Society through the suppression of private meetings owing to a fear of conspiracy; the failure, owing to the death of James I, of their schemes for a great literary academy, endowment of research, etc., and concluded by insisting that any true interpretation of the age must include these men.

April 10th.—Mr. F. J. Furnivall in the chair. Mr. F. A. Marshall read a paper "On the Tragedy of *Richard II*" (Egerton MS., 1694). The Egerton MS. contained fifteen plays, most of them written during the first forty years of the seventeenth century. The date of *Richard II*, however, was entirely a matter of conjecture, but it was certainly neither the one seen by Dr. Forman nor the one played in connection with the Essex Rebellion. From the nature and quantity of the marginal notes, stage directions, etc., it seemed clear that the MS. had been used as a playhouse copy. Mr. Marshall held that the play was written by an actor, or at least by one with a large experience of the stage, and also that it had probably been much "cut" by the actors themselves. It is very "close," full of movement and bustle, and without any poetic flights. Mr. Marshall read the opening scene to show the dramatic force and stir with which the play began, and passed on to the amusing scene between Woodstock and a "spruce courtier," interesting from its being an evident reminiscence of the "Orsic" scene in *Hamlet.* A study of the points of similarity in this play and Shakespeare's followed, with a summary of the metrical analysis, which yielded the following results: average of unstopped lines, one in nine; of double endings, one in six; of rhymed lines, one in seven. As to date, Mr. Marshall held it to be certainly later than Shakespeare.

In the discussion that followed, the Chairman said that he had not the least doubt that the play was written after Shakespeare's time. The date was not earlier than 1620. The Rev. W. A. Harrison concurred as to date, and supplemented Mr. Marshall's list of resemblances by many other parallelisms of ideas and in some cases of *ipsissima verba.* These parallelisms were not confined to *Richard II*, but were to be found in several other plays. He held that the writer had seen many of Shakespeare's plays and kept many passages in his memory (thus supporting Mr. Marshall's view that the writer was an actor), and he might even have seen the Folio.

---

NEW YORK SHAKESPEARE SOCIETY, May 5th.—The Society held its second meeting and completed its organization. On motion of the President, Mr. Morgan, the Society elected Mr. J. O. Halliwell-Phillipps its first honorary member. About two hundred members were proposed, to be acted upon at the next ensuing meeting. A committee on publication of papers was appointed, and, on suggestion of the President, the following, expressive of the liberal aims of the Society, was made the motto for its seal:

In brief, Sir, study what you most affect.—*Taming of Shrew* I, i, 40.

CHARLES C. MARBLE, Secretary.

# REVIEWS.

## SOME RECENT PAMPHLETS.

Mr. Halliwell-Phillipps' *Hand-List** is a volume that should be in the hands of every student. The great labor involved in forming a collection of such widely scattered material as illustrations of the life of Shakespeare would have deterred many a less enthusiastic scholar; but the very difficulties surrounding it have added to Mr. Halliwell-Phillipps' zeal, and in this catalogue he gives the result of his labors. The present collection is the second that he has formed; an earlier one, made in conjunction with the late Mr. W. O. Hunt, having been presented to Stratford-on-Avon. It is especially rich in engraved views of the Shakespearian localities, the Birth-Place and the Church being particularly full. The collection of maps is also large, including, among others, the first map of Warwickshire on which the roads are marked, Norden's original manuscript Plan of Middlesex, and an original Plan of Stratford, by Samuel Winter, of which only one other is known to exist. Equally remarkable is the collection of original colored drawings of the paintings in the Guild Chapel, and five very rare engravings of the Arches of Triumph erected in honor of the entry of James I into London, and under which there is authentic evidence that Shakespeare himself passed. Numerous other rare engravings are enumerated, of which the chief and the gem of the collection is the Droeshout Engraving in the original proof state before it was altered, and which is the only copy that has yet been noticed. The collection embraces, in addition, a large number of drawings, many of them very old and obtained from the most unexpected sources. There are also numerous drawings made by Mr. J. T. Blight, F. S. A., at Mr. Halliwell-Phillipps' request in 1862–1868, of objects many of which have since been either modernized or destroyed. The drawings are not the least of the benefits Mr. Halliwell-Phillipps has conferred upon Shakespearians, and while at present they cannot be considered the most valuable part of his collection, it is doubtful if—with the exception of some score or two of rarities—it includes many more interesting objects.

The tempest aroused by the recent attacks upon Mr. J. O. Halliwell-Phillipps concerning his relations with the Corporation of Stratford-on-Avon has by no means subsided, as his latest pamphlet† clearly shows.

* *A Hand-List of the Drawings and Engravings Illustrative of the Life of Shakespeare, Preserved at Hollingbury Copse, near Brighton.* Brighton: For private circulation only. 1884.

† *The Stratford Records and the Shakespeare Autotypes:* A Brief Review of Singular Delusions that are Current at Stratford-on-Avon. By the Supposed Delinquent. The Third Edition [20 February]. Brighton: 1884–1885.

The first edition was so masterly a defense that anything further seemed uncalled for. Yet not only has Mr. Halliwell-Phillipps' explanation not been accepted, as it should have been, but renewed attacks have been made upon him both by the Stratford papers and by Mr. Charles Flower, who has taken so prominent a part in the matter.

The difficulty between Mr. Halliwell-Phillipps and the Corporation had been disposed of by a resolution passed by the latter on January 4th, in which they complimented him on the value of his work and invited him to continue it. Accepting this resolution in the spirit in which it originated, Mr. Halliwell-Phillipps prepared to continue his work, and even expressed his willingness to do so with the conjunction of a committee, although he had always objected to such an arrangement. Yet scarcely had he renewed his labor when he learned that Mr. Charles Flower was operating against him in another quarter, and while it was a matter outside the Corporation, the nature of the case was such as would not permit of the two working together. Mr. Halliwell-Phillipps has, therefore, announced that his connection with Stratford-on-Avon has ceased, a conclusion to be regretted not only that so eminent a student should have met with difficulties and unkindness in the prosecution of his labors, but also because his opponents, instead of destroying his defense, are only satisfied with heaping additional abuse upon his head.

One of the most amusing skits suggested by the recent agitation over the proposed examination of Shakespeare's grave is the small pamphlet by Mr. Charles Jones.* The first portion, describing the theft of the skull by one Frank Chambers, a physician, originally appeared in the *Argosy* for October, 1879, but the second, describing the finding of the skull by the author, is first published in the present work. The book is well written and the story ingeniously told and well calculated to deceive the unsuspecting reader. We cannot pass the book without protesting against the bad taste displayed in the design of the cover—a cheap red, ornamented with a large skull. It seems odd that so careful a publisher as Mr. Stock should have issued so coarse-looking a pamphlet.

Mr. Rabone's pamphlet† is chiefly interesting to those familiar with the history of the Brooch—to which it is largely devoted—for the illustrations he gives of Luckenbooth Brooches of the sixteenth century, from the Natural Museum of the Society of Antiquaries of Scot-

* *How Shakespeare's Skull was Stolen and Found.* By a Warwickshire man. London, Elliott Stock, 1884.

†*A Lecture on Some Portraits of Shakespeare and Shakespeare's Brooch*, Delivered by Mr. John Rabone, to the Members of the Birmingham Natural History and Microscopical Society, November 15th, 1883. Reprinted, by request, from the *Birmingham Daily Gazette*, November 20th, 1883. With an Appendix and Illustrations. Birmingham, 1884.

land, Edinburgh. The brooches are most of them of the same general shape and style as Shakespeare's Brooch and are important—since their date is known with certainty to be of the sixteenth century—as showing that this style was current in Shakespeare's lifetime. Mr. Rabone's remarks on the portraits are, necessarily, limited, his discussion being confined to the Droeshout, Chandos, and Stratford portraits. He makes, however, a grievous slip of the pen when he speaks on page 6 of Dryden having known Shakespeare well.

Mr. Gould's brochure* is devoted to showing how bad is the accepted text of Shakespeare and to suggesting a great variety of improvements and changes in it. Unfortunately, the author fails to give any other reasons for his emendations other than that they seem to him better than the accepted readings, and his work, therefore, is of little practical value. Some of the points, however, are well taken and are quite ingenious, but the form in which they are presented to the public is such as to prevent their ever being accepted by the scholar.

Mr. King's reply to Mr. Norris' plea for the opening of Shakespeare's grave† is a vigorous and skillful defense of what may not unappropriately be termed the "orthodox" side of the case. It is refreshing to read so strong an argument after going through the mass of hypotheses advanced by the holders of the opposite course. It is a matter both of surprise and regret that the opening of the grave should have found the able and cultured advocates it has, but Mr. King handles his weapons with equal care, and while his pamphlet has had but a limited circulation, it must, nevertheless, be included among the most interesting contributions to the literature of the subject.

Equally pleasant reading is Mr. Dawson's brief study of the Bacon-Shakespeare Controversy.‡ The writer does not attempt an extended study of his subject, but in the briefest manner to tell "the origin of the theory that Shakespeare did not write Shakespeare, what the theory is, and suggest how you may decide the question for yourselves." This is done in an exceedingly interesting way, and the pamphlet will well repay reading.

Finally, there may be commended Professor Demmon's valuable reference list§ to the Sonnets, which, while confined to the books to

* *Corrigenda and Explanations of the Text of Shakespeare.* By George Gould. London, J. S. Virtue & Co., Limited, 1881.

*Ibid.* A New Issue. London, 1884.

† *Shall We Open Shakespeare's Grave?* No A Reply by Thomas D. King, to the Question put by Mr. J. Parker Norris in the July number of the *Manhattan.* Printed for private circulation only. Montreal, September, 1884.

‡ *The Bacon-Shakespeare Controversy:* A Paper Read before the First Congregational Literary and Social Club, Columbus, O., January 26th, 1885. By E. O. Dawson. Columbus, 1885.

§ *Course in English Masterpieces: References for the Use of Students.* By Isaac N. Demmon, A. M. Ann Arbor, October, 1884.

be found in the Macmillan Shakespeare Library, is sufficiently extensive to be of use to the general student. The references are both to English and German authors.

Mr. Norris' pamphlet on the Death Mask* should also be mentioned, and also—though very different in subject and style—Mr. Thompson's gay illustrations of the street parade of the Order of Cincinnatus last summer.†

---

## MISCELLANY.

Mr. Rolfe's lectures on Shakespeare before the New England Conservatory of Music are attracting unusual attention in Boston.

The brilliant open-air representation of *As You Like It*, in which Lady Archibald Campbell met with so distinguished success last summer, will be repeated this year. Nine dates have been selected, three each in May, June, and July, and both *As You Like It* and *The Faithfull Shepherdesse* will be given. The plays will be given under the patronage of the Prince and Princess of Wales.

Dr. Ingleby has prepared for publication the diary of Thomas Greene, Town Clerk at Stratford-on-Avon during the later years of Shakespeare's life. The volume, which is entitled *Shakespeare and the Welcombe Enclosures*, is a folio, with autotype reproductions of the diary, and includes an introduction by Dr. Ingleby, a transcript by Mr. Edward Scott, and an appendix of illustrative documents.

Early in June Dr. B. Rush Field will issue a second edition of his *Medical Thoughts of Shakespeare*, which has been greatly enlarged by the addition of new chapters on The Physician, Surgery, Physiology, Anatomy, and Pharmacy, and a variety of other subjects. A number of medical thoughts have also been added from other authors.

The most remarkable feature in the *Jahrbuch* of the Deutche Shakespeare-Gesellschaft is the lengthy paper on the Baconian Society and things Baconian by Professor F. A. Leo. It is noteworthy as showing the progress made by a theory whose defenders, only a short time ago, would not have been even mentioned, much less criticised, in so conservative a publication. Herr Cohn's valuable and thorough Bibliography fills forty-four pages.

James Rees, the dramatic critic and author, who was, perhaps, better known as "Colley Cibber," died in Philadelphia on April 29th.

* *The Death Mask of Shakespeare.* By J. Parker Norris. (One hundred and fifty copies privately reprinted from the February number of SHAKESPEARIANA.) Philadelphia, 1884.

† *A Dream of Shakespeare.* Peter G. Thompson. Cincinnati, 1884.

He was born in 1802, but it was not until 1842 that he published his first work, a volume entitled *The Dramatic Authors of America.* He was author of a number of other books and several plays, and was an intimate friend of Edwin Forrest. His *Life* of the great actor is his best known work.

The *Athenæum* announces the death of Mr. H. Halford Vaughan, who twenty-five years ago occupied a prominent place at the University of Oxford. He obtained the English Essay Prize in 1836, was Fellow of Oriel, and was Professor of Modern History from 1848 to 1858. In 1878 and 1881 he published two volumes of *New Readings and New Renderings of Shakespeare's Tragedies* which were remarkble for their boldness and ingenuity.

Two wooden structures designed to represent the proposed new vestry at the Church of the Holy Trinity, Stratford-on-Avon, have been placed, one on the north side of the choir and the other on the south side of the chancel, with a view of giving an idea of the appearance of the new building when finished. This is the first step that has been taken toward the restoration of the Church, which was noticed in a recent issue.

The last annual report of the Birmingham Shakespeare Memorial Library shows the total number of volumes to be six thousand seven hundred and eighty-two, of which six hundred and forty-eight were added during the past year, distributed as follows:—English, nine editions in forty-five volumes; separate plays, sixty-five volumes; Shakespeariana, two hundred and thirty-three; French, one hundred and twenty volumes; German, one hundred and twenty volumes; Bohemian, seven volumes; Croatian, one volume; Dutch, eight volumes; Finnic, one volume; Flemish, three volumes; Greek (Modern), five volumes; Icelandic, one volume; Italian, twenty-seven volumes; Polish, three volumes; Russian, one volume; Spanish, three volumes. The Library is now fully equal to that destroyed by fire in 1879 and contains a number of rare books not contained in the earlier collection.

Considerable interest has been manifested in Chicago over the finding of an alleged autograph of Shakespeare's by Mr. C. F. Gunther, a well-known collector of that city. The signature is pasted on a fly-leaf of a copy of the Second Folio formerly in the possession of the Rev. John Ward, who was Vicar of Stratford-on-Avon shortly after Shakespeare's death. While nothing can be said positively concerning its genuineness without examining the autograph itself, the circumstances of its discovery are not such as to give one a strong faith in it.

## HAY FEVER.

Once established, the return of Hay Fever is counted on at a fixed hour of the fatal day with the same certainty as the rising of the sun. And until it has run its course the words "endurance" and "patience" have to the sufferers an emphasis of meaning known to no others. Some persons are affected as early as in June, others as late as September. It is, like nasal catarrh, a disturbance of the mucous membrane, and its most appropriate title, perhaps, is "annual catarrh." It has been by some called "rose cold," "hay asthma," etc. Hundreds of our patients who have used "Compound Oxygen" report a removal of unhealthy conditions predisposing to catarrh and asthma and hay fever, and several who were at one time acute sufferers from hay fever report that they believe themselves to be entirely cured. The following letters are of especial interest to hay fever sufferers now looking forward with dread to the coming of their annual visitor. They have here an indication of a pleasant way to avoid the necessity of entertaining so unwelcome a guest.

A gentleman in Greenfield, Mass., wrote to us in regard to his wife. In stating her case he gave the following particulars:

"One year ago last spring she had rose or hay fever, which terminated in asthma, and was sick in bed most of the winter, with soreness of the chest, cough, and hard breathing. Coughs hard now and raises considerable, and is very thin and feeble. No strength and very little appetite."

The last report was at the end of six months. The following letter gives the patient's condition at the time it was written. Tracing the case along through the reports given, the change in six months was indeed "wonderful."

"To Drs. Starkey & Palen:

Dear Sirs:—My wife is, she says, well. A wonderful change in six months, from the bed to good health or nearly so, and all from Compound Oxygen.

"Has used nothing else. Appetite good, strength and flesh returning; everything looks like sound health again.

"We are grateful. Words cannot express the gratitude we owe you for this great cure."

A lady patient at Covert, Michigan, writes;

"It was very helpful in hay fever, and is the best remedy for colds or any lung trouble."

A physician at Newsom's Depot, Virginia, wrote in October, 1884:

"Having recommended your Compound Oxygen Treatment to my friend, E. M. D., of this place, and also his lady, who has been suffering for several years—himself fifteen years from the most trying and severe attacks every fall from 'hay fever,' his wife from chronic catarrh and bronchitis—both have experienced the greatest benefits, and especially Mr. D., who has entirely escaped his usual fall attacks, although he did not get your Treatment before it set in quite severely; yet in less than two weeks he was entirely relieved; to-day he tells me he is all right and well of it.

"So, having so greatly benefited them, I have determined to try it on two other of my patients at once. I write you to-day to get you to send me, per express, a complete outfit marked C. O. D. Send me also some of your treatises, pamphlets, and oblige. Should I again get the benefit I hope for and expect, you will hear from me again, and I shall think myself fortunate in finding so great a remedy among diseases that have always baffled our most skillful physicians."

In confirmation of the Doctor's statement about hay fever, we have a letter from Mr. D., the gentleman referred to, dated October 14, 1884, in which he says:

"I am much benefited. Have entirely escaped my usual attack of hay fever. Before I received the Compound Oxygen it had set in quite severely, yet in less than two weeks I was entirely relieved, and to-day am all right."

A letter of later date says;

"If you remember, I ordered of you a supply of your Compound Oxygen last August to use for hay fever and asthma myself, and for my wife, whose right lung was very much affected; in fact, she was given up at one time as having consumption. I think it did me more good than anything I ever used for hay fever, and now the doctor says my wife's lungs are all right; still, she takes it occasionally."

A patient in Oquawka, Illinois, who had suffered very much from hay fever, each fall, for five or six years, beginning the last week in July and lasting through August and September, last year used Compound Oxygen, and the good results attained led to other orders for Home Treatments from some of his acquaintances, though no direct report has been received from the patient himself.

The experience we have had satisfies us that almost every case of it may be cured. But it is of little use to expect that an attack can be stopped if the treatment be delayed until it is fully established.

To be surely successful, treatment should be commenced long enough before the expected invasion of the disease to have taken one full supply of Compound Oxygen—or two months.

Full directions will be given as to method of use. To any one wishing to learn, What Compound Oxygen Is; Its mode of Action and Results, a brochure of one hundred and eighty-eight pages, will be sent free, postpaid, on application. Address Drs. Starkey & Palen, 1109 and 1111 Girard Street, Philadelphia.

After July 1st, the address will be No. 1529 Arch Street, Philadelphia.